The Tall Tales of
Dracula's Daggers

The Return of the Count

The Tall Tales of
Dracula's Daggers

The Return of the Count

Gary Morecambe

SCHOLASTIC

Scholastic Children's Books,
Commonwealth House, 1–19 New Oxford Street,
London, WC1A 1NU, UK
A division of Scholastic Ltd
London ~ New York ~ Toronto ~ Sydney ~ Auckland
Mexico City ~ New Delhi ~ Hong Kong

First published in the UK by Scholastic Ltd, 2002

Text copyright © Gary Morecambe, 2002
Illustrations copyright © David Roberts, 2002

ISBN 0 439 98168 9

Printed and bound in Great Britain by Cox & Wyman Ltd, Reading, Berkshire

10 9 8 7 6 5 4 3 2 1

The right of Gary Morecambe and David Roberts to be identified respectively as the
author and illustrator of this work has been asserted by them in accordance with the
Copyright, Designs and Patents Act, 1988.

Deadication

For Countess Dereka of Brutonia

And not forgetting Natalya Angelica Lewis of Waleslovia

Contents

From the notes of
Professor Erich von Morcumstein

Dracula, the Lord of all Vampires. Known also as Vlad Basarab III, Vlad Dracul, Vlad Tepes (Vlad the Impaler). A fifteenth-century tyrannical ruler, who killed his enemies by impaling them on large sticks and then displayed their bodies outside his castle. When finally left to die in battle, it is said he whispered the words "One day I will return to torment the world."

Schleck's confusion turned to horror as the smoke took on a human form – his form…

✺ Chapter One
A Strange Reappearance

The shepherd tending his sheep on Mount Granu was finding it a particularly warm summer's evening. He couldn't recall the last time it had been so warm as to thaw the snow on the higher slopes of the Tryfool mountain range.

Following his cattle higher up the mountain, his attention was caught by a dull and dirty object lying in the grass. On first inspection, he couldn't make out what it was. But stooping to pick it up, he realized he was holding a dagger.

He scraped off some of the mud and grime to get a closer look. The dagger was inside a sheath covered in shiny jewels of different shapes and sizes. He pulled out the dagger, which was also covered in jewels. "This must be my lucky day," he thought. "Not only is it a beautiful dagger, but a very *valuable* one, I imagine. Certainly worth a few kronks." He looked furtively about the place, as if half-expecting someone to come and grab the dagger from him. But there was no one in sight. He took one last look before slipping the dagger in his overcoat pocket and getting on with tending his sheep. Soon he had forgotten all about it.

The shepherd, whose name was Schleck, lived alone in a tiny hut in the foothills. He never minded the loneliness, as he enjoyed his own company. If he was ever feeling *really* bored, he would talk to himself, or even his sheep. The great thing about talking to himself or to sheep, he had long ago discovered, was that he could discuss things without anyone ever disagreeing with him.

That evening, he had just finished his usual

supper of chopped vegetables when he suddenly remembered the dagger he had found earlier that day.

"Of course," he said suddenly. "It must still be in my coat pocket, where I left it. Fancy forgetting that beautiful thing!"

The dagger looked even more beguiling in the flickering light of the log fire. Fetching a handkerchief, he made himself comfortable in an armchair, and began polishing first the blade, then the hilt, where shone the beautiful jewels.

As he stroked his hand across the biggest jewel – a blood-red Burmese ruby – something strange happened. Smoke began to pour from its centre.

"What on earth...?" he began. But his confusion turned to horror as the smoke took on a human form – *his* form, right down to his ragged boots and unshaven face. It was as if someone had dropped a mirror right in front of him.

"Who... Who... Who...?" he began, but decided it was easier just to scream. Which he did. Loudly.

But his screams, though loud, were short-lived.

The stranger stepped towards the frightened shepherd and clicked his fingers once. In a flash the poor shepherd solidified. No longer was he flesh and blood, but cold, solid stone.

"Just like old times," grinned the stranger.

On the wall hung a small, cracked mirror. The stranger looked into it to examine his new form, but there was no reflection. He turned away from the mirror and examined his clothes and touched his hair – straggly, grey and unkempt, which hung down below his collar.

"I wait five years to return," he said, looking down at his attire, "and when finally I do, it is as a humble peasant. This is hardly a dignified return." He moved away from the mirror. "But this human form will have to suffice for the time being. At least it is a disguise." He took a deep breath. "When my strength is fully returned, I will surprise a few people who thought they'd seen the last of me. My former son, Rupert, is top of that list. Professor von Morcumstein; clever, but a meddling fool. That stupid policeman, Inspector Klaw. All of them. None will be spared."

He snatched the dagger from his unfortunate and extremely solid victim, then swept out of the hut and into the dark night.

Inspector Klaw was rummaging in his desk for a half-eaten sandwich when his office door opened a crack. A young sergeant appeared. "You have a visitor, sir."

"What sort of visitor?" asked Klaw.

"It's only me," said a voice, which was shortly joined by a body, as a rather tall man peered over the sergeant's shoulder. "I'm Randolph Klandou," said the man, who looked extremely uncomfortable in what the Inspector presumed were his "Sunday best" clothes.

Klaw gave his sergeant an exasperated look. "Couldn't this matter have been dealt with at the reception desk?"

"The, er, gentleman didn't stop at the reception desk, sir."

"I won't take much of your time, Inspector," said the visitor.

"Very well," sighed Klaw, hoping he meant what he said. Klaw had a particularly pressing day ahead of him. The sergeant shrugged, then left the office.

"I'm a shepherd," explained Randolph Klandou, once they were alone.

Klaw re-examined his visitor's clothing. "I had guessed as much."

"Ah. These smart clothes don't fool you detective

sorts," chuckled Klandou. "The thing is," he went on, "I keep a flock on the Radau side of the Tryfoolian range. The other night I thought I'd visit my neighbour, Schleck. It gets a bit lonely up there sometimes. We like to keep in touch when we. . ."

"To the point, Mr Klandou, if you please," said Klaw, trying very hard not to sound too impatient.

"Oh yes. Well, I dropped in last night, and guess what?"

"He was out?" suggested Klaw.

"In a manner of speaking," replied Klandou. "He was sitting by the embers of a fire not moving. At first I thought he was dead."

Klaw sighed impatiently. "Excuse my interruption, but why have you come to my department over this matter? There are three other police departments between here and the Radau side of the Tryfools."

"Oh, I tried the others, sir," replied the shepherd, leaning across the desk with a knowing glint in his eye. "Thing is, sir, they told me about you."

"Told you what?" asked Klaw, uncomfortably.

"About you and your previous dealings, some five or so years back. Dealings, shall we say, with those who aren't exactly alive, but not exactly dead, either."

Klaw felt a tingling sensation down his spine. This was one of the first references to the Krinkelfiend vampire case since the matter had been closed half a decade ago. He coughed nervously, and Klandou took it as the cue to continue his little story.

"My friend Schleck was frozen solid, as though he'd been carved from a large piece of stone."

Klaw's eyes widened. He remembered how Count Arnold Krinkelfiend had turned King Konstantine, the princess and the whole of their staff into stone statues at Viktoria Palace. Afterwards, Count Krinkelfiend's own kindly son, Rupert, chased the count across the snow-covered Tryfoolian mountains to try to retrieve the powerful dagger that had once belonged to Count Dracula. Rupert had discovered his father hiding in a cave and had cleverly outwitted him. The count had met his death through the vampire curse – daylight – and the dagger had been buried in a fortuitous avalanche. Or so they'd thought...

"I think," said the Inspector, rising to his feet, "you should take me to Mr Schleck's hut in the mountains. But first I need to make a few calls."

Inspector Klaw was pleased to see Rupert outside Schleck's mountain hut, as he approached the tiny dwelling with the shepherd Klandou. Rupert had been his first telephone call.

"It's been a long time, Inspector," said Rupert, shaking Klaw by the hand.

Klaw's warm smile on seeing his old friend evaporated when he went inside and saw the stone figure of Schleck sitting in an armchair.

"What do you make of this?" asked Klaw.

"Well," said Rupert, "not many people get turned to stone these days. Unless, of course, Father is up to his tricks again."

"Krinkelfiend back from the dead?" said Klaw. "But how?" He had grown accustomed to bizarre happenings where vampires were involved, but this was the most bizarre yet.

"It's unbelievable, I know," said Rupert. "But it *has* to be Father. I assumed the daylight had killed him, but what if it didn't? After all, we don't understand the mysteries of the dagger. I can only guess that it protected him somehow; swallowed his spirit. And now he has managed to escape from it and returned to get revenge."

"Which means," sighed Klaw, "he will probably have the dagger with him."

"What a nightmare for us all if we are right about this," said Rupert.

"But why turn this shepherd to stone?" asked Klaw, touching Schleck's solid surface.

"That's what I want to know," said Klandou.

"Other than the fact that such things amuse Father," said Rupert, "it is most likely he did it to take this poor man's identity."

"Two Schlecks?" said Klaw. "This one, and one walking around looking like Schleck, who is actually Krinkelfiend?"

"That's right, Inspector," sighed Rupert. "Though I doubt he'll stay around these parts very long. If he does have the dagger, he'll want to go where he feels safe."

"And where would that be?" asked Klaw.

"Bran," said Rupert. "Where Dracula's castle is. After all, it is Dracula's dagger he has, and if it can bring Father back to life, it could…"

"Bring Dracula back to life," finished Klaw, glumly. "Then we really *are* in trouble."

Rupert nodded. "I would like to say otherwise," he said, "but I think you are quite right, Inspector. We *are* in trouble." After a pause he asked, "What do you propose we do next?"

"I rang Professor von Morcumstein before coming here," said Klaw. "He'll be in Grund by the morning."

"Er, what about my friend Schleck?" asked Klandou.

"I'm afraid that until I find my father, your friend will have to remain as he is," said Rupert.

Professor Erich von Morcumstein, academic and renowned vampire theorist, was hurriedly packing his much-travelled case at his home in Muhlhausen.

"Most interesting!" he said to himself. "So it seems that Count Krinkelfiend is back among us. It is as I would have expected from a dagger of mystical powers, made for Vlad Dracula. Krinkelfiend will not be in the best frame of mind, particularly regarding those whom he will consider to be his enemies." He paused to add another item to his case. "I was so hoping to get another chance to see the dagger," he muttered cheerfully. "And now it seems that I just might."

Count Arnold Krinkelfiend, still travelling towards Transylvania, knew an attempt to find him would not be long in coming, once the stone occupant of that lonely mountain hut were discovered. It would become necessary for him to discard his current disguise for something less obvious. He wanted his journey to Transylvania to go as smoothly and quietly as possible.

Had his powers been fully restored, he could have taken on his original form – or, better still, the form of a bat, which would have meant he could have flown to the castle in style. But after more than five years of painfully slow regeneration, his powers were limited. He was like a battery that needed recharging, and to do this he wished to be in the safe surrounds of his hero's, and his own, homeland.

On leaving Gertcha, the count had taken a train journey in a southwesterly direction, terminating at Sucevita, which lies in the foothills of the Carpathian mountains. He had travelled second class on the overnight journey, blending in with a handful of travelling peasants who, fortunately, did not appear to know the shepherd Schleck.

He left the station at Sucevita, about half his journey to Bran in Transylvania completed. The first grey light of an approaching dawn was visible on the horizon, and the journey had weakened him. He needed to find somewhere safe to rest.

In Sucevita, one of the first people Count Krinkelfiend came across was a tramp. Krinkelfiend at once turned him to stone and stole his likeness. It was clever to take a fresh disguise, particularly that of a tramp, whom no one was going to miss or pay much attention to. It reminded him of the time he had transformed into Walter, King Konstantine's head servant. Through the disguise he had managed to take control of Viktoria Palace. The memories of that time suddenly came flooding back. He remembered his hopeless employees – Vermyn and his underlings, Itch and Scratch – and felt they had all let him down badly.

"I will acquire new and better servants when I reach Bran," he muttered to himself. But most of all he thought of his former son, Rupert. He looked forward to exacting revenge on the one who had tried to destroy him in the Tryfoolian mountains.

Dawn was just beginning to break but Krinkelfiend had finally found what he was looking for – a house seemingly no different from the others, except that to one side there was a tiny window which peered in on a basement room. Very easy to break in to.

Soon he was in a dark, mouldy cellar, full of wooden barrels of home-made wine, and scattered tables and sacks. He managed to shift one large pile of sacks and scrambled quickly beneath them, burying himself in complete and joyous darkness. "I dislike daylight more than ... more than ... more than my enemies," he at last thought. He smiled to himself and shut his eyes. Suspended death soon overcame him, from which he would not emerge until the sun had completed its cycle and glorious night had fully returned.

The most terrifying vision appeared: a giant white stallion ridden by an equally giant Count Krinkelfiend...

✎ Chapter Two
Helsing, and a Frightening Attack

The following night, a tramp with a few fleas and a limp surveyed the once-great castle from the cover of the trees that lay at its foundations. If the tramp had possessed a working heart, it would have been rapidly pounding in excitement. Here he was, Arnold Krinkelfiend, about to cross the threshold of the home of the lord of all vampires once more.

"I return to my master's home. And soon," thought Krinkelfiend, "my master will occupy it once more. Then he will reign supreme."

He rubbed his thin bony hands together. "Time to take a little stroll around the old place," murmured Krinkelfiend. "Let's see how you have fared down the centuries."

He began to scramble up a slope which led to one of many entrances. He stopped to glance back on the sleepy town, and sniffed at the air. "I sense old enemies," he said through narrow lips. "Already my powers are beginning to return. I must make sure that some harm comes to those who hunt me. It would be impolite not to acknowledge their arrival."

Once inside the castle, Krinkelfiend began to move around with purpose gleaming in his narrow eyes. "Where did our lord and master hide you, Orlov?" he said aloud. "If you had been *my* servant, where would I have put you?"

Eventually, Krinkelfiend found an underground passage that led to a very cold and damp cellar. "Ah yes!" he smiled as he stepped into the room and saw what it was that made the room so cold.

On a large stone table rested an equally large block of ice. Inside the ice was the vague shape of a man. "Orlov!" stated Krinkelfiend, excitedly. "What magic to keep the ice from ever melting. The magic of our master."

But Krinkelfiend, though strong in his praise of Dracula's magic, knew that it was a simple enough spell to break, and duly did so. With a click of his fingers, the ice began to fall apart in dripping clumps, until the defrosted body of Orlov rolled to the floor.

"OUCH!" said Orlov, Dracula's one-time servant, clambering painfully to his knees.

Orlov was a dreadfully deformed man. He had ten fingers and toes, but sadly on each hand and foot. His nose was so broken that it pointed away from his face at right angles. Whenever he tried to smell his supper, he could only smell the supper of whoever was seated next to him. He was short and dumpy and walked with a limp because his right leg was three inches longer than his left leg.

"My dear Orlov," said Krinkelfiend. "I had forgotten how truly ugly and deformed you are. How splendid to meet you again."

"And it's good to see you, too," said Orlov huffily, only too aware of his ugliness.

"Ah, so you remember me?" said Krinkelfiend proudly.

"No!"

"Well, you will do," said Krinkelfiend, with a dangerous edge to his voice. "I am Count Arnold Krinkelfiend. I once knew your master – *our* master. I have come to return him to us. And you, Orlov, are to be my servant till he returns. That is why, I imagine, he froze you in ice. One day, he knew he would come back."

"If you're Krinkelfiend," said Orlov pointing a finger at him, "then why is it that you're dressed as a tramp?"

"I'm glad the centuries spent in frozen isolation haven't totally damaged what little brain you possess, Orlov," said Krinkelfiend. "Today I might appear to the world as a tramp, but this very night I shall reinstate my true self."

"You certainly talk like a count," admitted Orlov, struggling to his feet. "Ooh, these old legs. Give us a hand, will you?"

"I do not give servants a hand," snarled Krinkelfiend. "And if you wish to remain unfrozen," he went on, "then you will serve me, and serve me well." With that, Krinkelfiend clicked his fingers and Orlov found himself floating around the room, completely weightless.

"HELP!"

"Certainly," said Krinkelfiend, clicking his fingers again. Orlov fell to the ground in a painful heap.

"I am here to serve you, Count," bowed Orlov once he'd managed to get to his wobbly feet.

"That's better," said Count Krinkelfiend. "What fun we are going to have together, Orlov," he said, rubbing his hands.

"Yes. What fun!" said Orlov, doubtfully.

It was with relief and nervous excitement that Professor von Morcumstein and his colleagues, Inspector Klaw and Rupert Krinkelfiend, checked into a hotel in the town of Bran. They had passed the long journey from Grund discussing the worrying possibility that Count Arnold Krinkelfiend was alive, and trying to guess what he was up to *this* time.

Later that day, they assembled in Rupert's room to make a plan. Even in the fading light, it was evident that Dracula's castle dominated Bran. Fifteenth-century peasants had taken four years to build the castle by hand, and it showed in the sheer quality and size of the structure.

"We must go to Bran church," Rupert told them. "Many years ago, I knew a man who had been employed as a cleaner at the church and who knew of my vampire background without fearing it. He and my father were sworn enemies. But I liked him. He was always kind to me. He seemed to accept vampires as part of Transylvanian life. I feel sure he would know if there have been any strange goings-on around here lately."

"Very well," said the professor. "If this man was a friend, and if we can find him, it sounds a good starting place."

"Perhaps he was a vampire," suggested Inspector Klaw.

"Oh, no," said Rupert, firmly shaking his head. "There's much to him that would surprise you, and in the fullness of time you may learn all about his fascinating history, but he is no vampire. Believe me, he is anything *but* a vampire."

The church was, in fact, a huge Gothic cathedral full of grandeur and foreboding.

"An inspiring place to be when in search of a vampire," remarked Klaw, just as a four-thousand-pipe organ boomed out music by Bach, which echoed hauntingly off the enormously tall walls.

"A sombre piece of music to welcome us," commented the professor, as he looked around at the magnificent stained-glass windows, depicting various Biblical scenes.

Klaw shuddered as he moved down the long flagstoned aisle, which divided rows and rows of empty pews. There were little clusters of people at prayer in the front pews, but it was such a vast cathedral that the three men felt quite alone.

"Over there, gentlemen," said Rupert, nodding at a man sweeping a portion of the floor near a vestry entrance.

"Excuse me," said Rupert, trying to make himself heard above the organ music. The cleaner, who was a young man, glanced their way. "Does Helsing still work here?"

"Helsing? No," said the cleaner, leaning thoughtfully on his broom. "He retired years ago. He must be over ninety years of age."

"I see. Thank you," said Rupert, unable to hide his disappointment as they turned to leave.

"Wait a bit," said the cleaner. "That doesn't mean you can't see him."

They stopped and turned around. "This building was Helsing's life," explained the cleaner. "He visits every day, usually in the evening. In fact, he should be here now. It's on his way home from the inn, you see."

"Fine," smiled Rupert. "We'll wait."

They didn't have to wait long. Five minutes later, shuffling footfalls could be heard making their way down the aisle.

"Helsing!" whispered Rupert. Then louder: "HELSING!"

The very old man, hunched and weary, approached the small group. "Rupert! Can it really be you?" he said, overjoyed at seeing the young Krinkelfiend. "It is so good to see you again after all these years."

"And you too, Helsing, and you too," smiled Rupert, shaking the man's hand warmly. "Allow me to introduce my friends. This is the eminent Professor von Morcumstein."

"Pleased to meet you, sir," said Helsing. "Your reputation precedes you."

"And this is Inspector Klaw of the Gertcha police department."

"Delighted, I'm sure," bowed Helsing. "Well, what brings you all here, gentlemen?"

"I suppose," answered Rupert, "that has a lot to do with Father."

"Ah," nodded Helsing, knowingly.

"Have you noticed anything strange happening in Bran recently?" Rupert asked him.

"Bran has always been a bit of a strange place,"

sighed Helsing, "but, yes – certain inexplicable things have been occurring."

"Such as?" pressed Inspector Klaw.

"Such as a strange disturbance in the graveyard outside this very church only last night," whispered Helsing, coughing a few times as he spoke.

"A disturbance, you say?" said Klaw.

Helsing looked at the three of them carefully. "Come with me to the vestry. It is more private for a conversation of this nature."

Once they were inside the small room, Helsing closed and bolted the door behind them, and they all sat down.

Rupert sighed a sad little sigh. "We think it's Father," he said. "He's on the loose with a rather dangerous dagger. You know about these things, Helsing. It's Dracula's legendary dagger."

"I see," said the old man nodding glumly. "I had guessed something of this sort must have happened."

"And we believe," added Rupert, "that he could be here as some kind of servant to Dracula."

"Yes. Why else would he come here?" shrugged

Helsing. "Now, let me tell you about life in Bran, as it is at the moment. I left the inn late last night, and the route home takes me past the graveyard," he explained. "As I made my way, I heard a peculiar grating sound – the sound of stone rubbing against stone. I stopped to look, and to my amazement saw the stone covers on top of some of the tombs sliding back, all by themselves. I watched in horror as the occupants climbed out of their graves and walked away towards the woods."

"Why the woods, I wonder?" asked Inspector Klaw.

"Dracula's castle lies just beyond them," explained Rupert.

"And now you tell me your father has the dagger," said Helsing. "Bodies leaving their graves; Count Krinkelfiend in possession of possibly the most powerful object on the planet. Something is happening which involves Dracula. Krinkelfiend is doing something for Dracula."

"Preparing a way for his return to life?" suggested the professor.

"Possibly," nodded Helsing. "These Undead

figures from the graveyard would make useful servants to Dracula. In time, he could create an army of them."

"Though whether it is Dracula or Father who is bringing the dead to life remains to be seen," said Rupert. "Personally, I agree with the professor. I think it is Father preparing the way for Dracula. He always likes to be a step ahead of everyone."

"You mentioned an army," Klaw said to Helsing. "Why would he need an army?"

Helsing chuckled softly. "My dear Inspector, throughout his whole bloodthirsty history, Dracula has always been supported by an army. His armies waged war on other armies. He didn't acquire the nickname Vlad the Impaler through a kindly respect for his enemies... However," he added, "this particular army of Undead recruits can only operate at night, as any vampire himself can only operate at night. Still, an army it remains."

"And with this nocturnal army," continued Rupert, "he can destroy life in Bran, then other towns and villages, until he is commanding a mighty, lifeless force, which will eventually take over the world. And that, Inspector, will be his work."

"But that would take him years and years to achieve," said Klaw.

"I mentioned before that time is not a consideration to a vampire," Rupert reminded him. "Even if it takes him a hundred years, he will slowly and inevitably move towards his goal."

"Unless he is stopped, of course," pointed out the professor.

"Although the work may have begun, I do not believe Dracula is back among us yet," said Rupert confidently. "One thing I have found in recent times is that despite the dwindling of my powers, my sense of vampire presence is as strong as ever."

"Maybe we can come up with a plan if we all put our minds together," said Helsing, with a warm smile. "But listen, it is dangerous to act during the night. You would be wise to stay in your rooms during the dark hours and confine your movements to daylight, when no harm can come to you."

"You're quite right," said Rupert. "Come, gentlemen. Let us return to the warmth and safety of our hotel. It is already getting late."

They left the vestry and made their way into the main gallery of the cathedral. Their footfalls echoed as they marched solemnly towards the doors, Helsing following close behind. But before they were even halfway down the aisle, a thunderous crash sounded in their ears, and sheets of fragmenting glass exploded from the arched windows and poured down on them.

"Take cover," cried Klaw, hurling himself under one of the pews.

More windows imploded, and they watched from relative safety as the most terrifying vision any of them had ever witnessed appeared: a giant white stallion ridden by an equally giant Count Krinkelfiend dressed as a fifteenth-century soldier in full battle gear.

The monstrous apparition roared with bitter laughter as it floated around the cathedral, destroying everything in its path.

"We have to get out of here," cried Rupert, as a pile of psalm books hurtled towards his head.

Others who were in the cathedral were thinking the same thing, and people were screaming, shouting, running. But those fortunate enough to reach the main doors unscathed were making a frightening discovery: a strange, invisible force was pushing them back, keeping them just out of reach of their escape route.

Rupert's brain was working quickly. He knew that this grandiose exhibition by his father was designed to shock and scare them. If he had wanted them dead, he would surely have gone about it in a more practical fashion. All the same, it was a very dangerous situation, and one they were keen to escape.

"HELSING!" shouted Rupert. "Is there another way out?"

"Follow this pew to the end," croaked Helsing. "There is a side door there. It is always left unlocked."

As they crawled along the side of the pew, the

gale and the bitter laughter intensified. "FOOLS!" shouted the count. "You thought you had seen the last of me, but I am back and I will squash you like insects!"

With that about fifty hymn books pelted them on their retreating backs. Krinkelfiend saw that they were making for a door, so cut off their path to it by placing himself in the way.

"Now what?" said Rupert.

Inspector Klaw had a brainwave. He noticed a tall silver crucifix standing by the altar. Flinging himself over three rows of pews, he sprinted for it, clenched it in his fist, and tossed it at Krinkelfiend, all in one motion.

"AAARGH!" screamed the vampire in agony, the crucifix burning right through his skin. He kicked his stallion and flew from the cathedral as quickly as he'd come, and just as quickly all was silent in the carnage.

"Most impressive," panted the professor, going over to congratulate Klaw. "You remembered that vampires cannot bear the touch – barely even the sight – of a crucifix."

"*And* garlic," added Klaw teasingly.

"My goodness," smiled the professor, "you'll soon be more knowledgeable than me."

"Well, Father's had his fun for the evening," said Rupert, as the professor and Klaw rejoined them, "so proving he is as unbalanced as he ever was."

"He was playing with us," said the professor, more curious than concerned.

"If that was playing, I wouldn't like to see him when he was after us for real," said Klaw.

"This is bad – very bad," tutted Helsing, after Rupert had helped him to his tired legs. "Your father is very angry with you."

"Well, I *did* try to kill him when he was in the Tryfoolian mountains," said Rupert. "I had to. He had Dracula's dagger and would have taken over the world."

"I understand what you had to do," said Helsing. "And I can see why he is so angry. Though at the moment it appears he is merely enjoying himself: a cat with mice, so to speak."

"Even if it's just his little game," said Rupert, "I've never seen him so powerful before. It's strange considering what he has been through of late."

"Nothing is strange while he holds the dagger, my boy. He could go from being in a very weakened state to one of great power, if he has some basic knowledge of the dagger."

"How do you know all this?" asked Klaw, suspiciously.

"It... It is a sort of hobby of mine. The history of Vlad Dracula," Helsing said quickly.

"Helsing is a remarkable man," said Rupert, hoping that would put an end to too many questions. Rupert knew that Helsing would tell the others more about his remarkable life when he felt the time was right.

"What is the best way out of here?" he asked him.

"Just follow this passage and it will lead you into the graveyard. From there you will be able to see the gaslights on the main street."

"And what of you?"

"I think it will be safe enough for me to stay here," shrugged Helsing. "It would appear your father has had his fun and gone away for the time being. And anyway," he added, "someone must try to explain what has happened and assist in the tidying up."

"We can help you with that," offered Klaw.

"No, no, Inspector," said Helsing. "I think for now you gentlemen have enough to concern yourselves with. But I will be in touch."

The second they were outside, Rupert realized they were not alone. He nudged Inspector Klaw, who nudged the professor.

The three men stared ahead at ten indistinct figures standing motionless before them.

"Can we be of assistance?" Rupert asked. At once this seemed to trigger a reaction and the figures began to stumble towards them. Instinctively, Rupert pulled his friends closer to the wall of the cathedral.

"Who are they?" whispered Klaw, but his question was soon answered as their awful features became illuminated by the fractured light pouring through the shattered windows of the cathedral.

The figures all wore rags and were in an advanced state of decomposition.

"The Undead," whispered the professor, almost cheerfully.

Rupert strained his eyes beyond them, and saw several tombs opening as more of the Undead joined in the chase.

"Time to leave," said Rupert. "Head for the wood. It'll give us some cover." The three men sprinted along the edge of the cathedral and dived into the trees.

"Surely we need to get to the road?" panted the professor.

"Right now, we just need to get anywhere that's away from *them*!" said Rupert, pointing over his shoulder, as the rotting bodies pursued them relentlessly.

"What about your vampire powers?" asked Klaw. "Couldn't you do some of the magic we saw you do at Viktoria Palace?"

"That was five years ago, Inspector," sighed Rupert. "I haven't used them since. We have to accept that I have as much chance as you two of stopping these creatures."

"Let's get up one of these trees then," suggested Klaw. No one needed a moment to consider the idea, though the professor found the climb a most difficult one.

The three men huddled in branches high in the tree and waited. The silent figures beneath walked blindly on, oblivious to their prey looking down on them from high above.

"Do you think it's safe to climb down?" whispered the professor, after five minutes had elapsed. "It's most uncomfortable up here."

"Let's give it a bit longer," said Rupert. "Just so we can be sure."

"I doubt they'll return to the graveyard for some while," remarked the professor.

"Why is that?" asked Klaw.

The professor nodded towards the castle.

"You are right," nodded Rupert. "It wasn't just for our benefit that these grisly creatures made their appearance this evening. According to Helsing, they did the same thing last night. They'll be gathering at Castle Bran to receive instructions from Father." After a short pause he added, "Father really is such a nuisance at times."

"To put it mildly," said Klaw.

"You two should get back to the hotel right away," said Rupert.

"And what of you?" asked the professor.

"You don't intend going to the castle alone – tonight?" said Klaw, guessing that that was *exactly* Rupert's plan.

"I feel it's as good a time as any," said Rupert. "Unless I spy on Father we're not going to find out very much about what he has planned – not until it is too late. If I'm careful, I should be safe."

"On the other hand, you might get yourself into all kinds of trouble," said Klaw. "He wasn't exactly concerned about your well-being the last time you confronted each other, and I'm sure he won't have forgiven you for spoiling his plans. And now, it appears, he is more powerful than ever."

Rupert shrugged his shoulders. "It is my intention to spoil his plans again, Inspector. He's *my* father. Whether he likes it or not, I am his only child, and in a way I feel responsible for him. But don't worry. I'll take great care and I'll report back in the morning."

Rupert leaped from the tree and was swiftly swallowed up by the darkness.

"Come on, Professor," sighed Klaw. "Let's return to the hotel."

Orlov peeled back the dome-shaped lid with a flourish.
"Voila! One Goat's Head Surprise."

☙ Chapter Three
An Audience with the Dead

Rupert kept clear of the main thoroughfares on his short but arduous journey to Castle Bran. He tried turning into a bat, but it was hopeless. Five years of vampire inactivity and daily exposure to daylight had left him powerless.

It worried him that this giant old castle was so quiet. He had expected to hear some chanting or see some of his father's Undead friends marching around. Instead, he found the castle grounds still and seemingly empty.

"If they are not here," he said aloud, "then they must be. . ." his eyes fell upon a trapdoor on the ground, right beside a well, ". . .underground!"

Rupert lifted the trap door and stared into the pit of darkness below. "Here goes!" he sighed, and he climbed down some steps which led to a long, dank tunnel. He followed the tunnel, which appeared endless, as it ran deep beneath the foundations of Castle Bran. The darkness didn't bother him – that, at least, was one vampire trait that had remained.

At last, the tunnel came to an abrupt halt by a huge wooden door. Rupert opened it cautiously and peered inside. On the other side of the door was a vast crypt – an enormous stone room which looked a bit like a wine cellar but without the wine. Rupert sneaked inside and hid behind a large grey pillar that supported the crumbling ceiling.

He saw he was not alone. In the cellar stood some fifty of the Undead. They waited silently; expectantly. Their empty gaze was fixed on a plinth in front of them.

A gust of wind, an explosion of purple smoke, and there on the plinth in front of his sickly-looking flock, stood the count.

"Good evening, ladies and gentlemen," he hissed in a deep tone. He was no longer dressed as a fifteenthth-century soldier, but in his favourite long black tails with a black top hat upon his narrow head. The hat made him look exceptionally tall and frightening, as did his transparent complexion and long bony fingers from which grew equally long, pointed nails.

No spoken response came from the lifeless group.

"The time is fast approaching when we shall begin to visit the homes of the human residents of Bran," he told them. "One by one we shall transform them into our own likeness. This will be done very easily. You are the indestructible force of Vlad Tepes: nothing and no one can stop you from your task." He tapped his chest a couple of times. "I, Count Arnold Krinkelfiend, servant to Vlad Tepes, have given you the power of the vampire bite. An incision to the neck of your intended victim by your incisors will bring death, yet, at the same time, new, everlasting life. They, too, will then serve me faithfully and unquestioningly, and together, when our lord and master is returned, we will conquer the world."

As he spoke, all those gathered snarled to reveal razor-sharp teeth behind rotting gums.

"And now, my children of the night, you will return to the graveyard," said Count Krinkelfiend. "Tomorrow night at this time, you will reassemble here, and so will begin the new reign of Vlad Tepes. Go now, my children."

The figures turned in slow, robotic movements, and headed for the tunnel.

Rupert, who had stayed long enough to hear his father's words, had made his way to the tunnel's mouth and was about to sprint away in the opposite direction when his cloak caught on the hinge of the door. It delayed him just a few moments, but it was enough for those Undead nearest him to stretch out their arms and grab him.

"Aaarggh!" was all Rupert managed to say, before being dragged back into the crypt.

Krinkelfiend, meanwhile, was some distance

away, at the front of the room and deep in conversation with Orlov.

"The get-together seemed to go well, Master," grovelled Orlov, hobbling behind the vampire as he proudly strutted around the crypt.

"Yes, Orlov," said Krinkelfiend, without looking upon the face of the ugly servant. "And tomorrow is the beginning of the end for life on this planet as everyone has come to know and accept it. Tomorrow we begin summoning our lord and master. That makes me most glad."

As he turned to leave, there was a rustling from the doorway. The Undead rolled into the crypt once more. "What is the matter?" barked Krinkelfiend. "I said, come back tomorrow night. Why do you return now?"

The Undead shuffled forwards and dumped poor Rupert at his father's feet. "Er... Good evening," gulped Krinkelfiend's unfortunate offspring.

Krinkelfiend's face showed little emotion, other than a slight flicker in one eye. "Well, well, well," he said. "Good evening, my former son. An unexpected, though delightful, pleasure." He waved a hand at the Undead without taking his narrowed gaze from Rupert, and they turned and shuffled silently back towards the tunnel.

"How have you been keeping?" said Rupert, struggling to his feet.

His father laughed in a menacing and altogether unpleasant fashion. "Considering you tried to kill me some years ago, I am keeping remarkably well, thank you."

Krinkelfiend casually examined the chain watch which hung from his waistcoat. "I wouldn't dream of sending you back to the village at this hour," he said. "And I'm sure you would like to see around the castle. I assume that is why you are here? And your friends? How are they?"

"They are very well, Father," said Rupert, going along with his father in not mentioning their encounter at the cathedral. "And yes; I would very much like a tour of your castle." All Rupert could think at that moment was that he must keep his father calm. Should he say anything that might annoy him, then Rupert would certainly never feel the sun on his face again. Then, when the chance to escape presented itself, he would leave without a goodbye.

"You have lost your transparent complexion," remarked Krinkelfiend. "How sad. Such a shame we are so different from each other."

"Not that different," said Rupert. "We both managed to escape from the Tryfoolian mountains. By the way, how *did* you manage that?"

"My escape?" smiled Krinkelfiend. "The dagger protected me. You and your clever professor misread the outcome. The dagger needed to feed off my powers to enhance its own powers – very necessary in our final resuscitation of Dracula. I was turned to dust, but the dagger consumed the dust and made me whole again. I was trapped within the dagger, until..." he paused.

"Yes?" encouraged Rupert, who knew his father was never happier than when discussing the dagger.

"Until some peasant who had found the dagger rubbed the ruby," explained Krinkelfiend. "That freed me. And now you see before you a vampire ten times the vampire you left for dead on the snowy and extremely chilly slopes of the Tryfool.

Though I admit that fortune was on my side," he added. "If it hadn't been for the warmer weather, the snow would not have melted. . ."

"And you and the dagger would have remained buried?"

"Precisely, my former son."

Krinkelfiend stared deeply into his son's eyes. "And now I, too, find myself asking a question. What brings my former son to Bran Castle? Why has he been following me for several days and nights?"

Rupert was about to point out that that was two questions, but not wanting to be atomized on the spot, decided to let it pass.

"I heard you were in the vicinity," he told the count. "I thought I should pay you a call."

"Oh, really?" grinned Krinkelfiend. "A very *sneaky* call, I must say. And your clever friend, Professor von Morcumstein? And I mustn't forget our upholder of the law; the intrepid Inspector Klaw of the Gertcha police department. You appear to have left them behind. Maybe they are planning my destruction this very moment. But that is an unreasonable thought, I'm sure. Tut, tut."

He clicked his fingers and part of one wall slid back to reveal a small stone stairway. "I'm sure we can find much to talk about, and the night is yet young. Let us partake of wine in my private quarters. It is so dreary down here in the crypt."

Rupert was not in any position to refuse. "At least," he thought, "I'll get the chance to see exactly what Father is up to."

From the crypt, Krinkelfiend led Rupert to a dining room of gigantic proportions.

Father and son sat at either head of an extremely long table. Rupert hoped he wouldn't be asked to pass the salt and pepper: it would be a long walk.

"So, my disappointing and disappointed former son," called out Krinkelfiend. "Do you like my dining arrangements?"

"Most satisfactory, Father," Rupert called back.

"There is no need for the word Father," said Krinkelfiend a little moodily. "*Former* father is acceptable. I thought it was understood that *that* part of our relationship was at an end." He paused a moment, then snapped his fingers. Orlov appeared, bearing a large silver tray. On top of the silver tray was a large silver lid.

Krinkelfiend eyed the approaching manservant with open eagerness. "What delights have you rustled up for us this evening, Orlov?"

"Nothing too grand, Count," replied Orlov, bashfully. "Goat's Head Surprise. I hope you approve."

The vampire chuckled with hungry anticipation. "My dear little and grossly deformed Orlov, you know I simply adore Goat's Head Surprise."

"Goat's Head Surprise?" queried Rupert from way down the other end of the table. "I don't recall you eating that when we lived together. What is it, exactly?"

"But my dear former child, if you knew then there would be no surprise," explained Krinkelfiend.

"Oh, right," said Rupert, a little anxiously.

Orlov peeled back the dome-shaped lid with a flourish. "*Voila!* One Goat's Head Surprise."

Even seated so far away, Rupert could soon see why the dish was so named. On the silver plate the two ghastly eyes of this particular goat's head stared across the table at him. They blinked a few times before rolling around to take a look at firstly Orlov, then Krinkelfiend. The goat made a bleating noise which was curtailed by Orlov slamming the lid back down.

Rupert felt positively sick.

"I do so like my food to be fresh," remarked Krinkelfiend, with a wry smile.

"I prefer mine to be silent," said Rupert.

"My dear Rupert," said Krinkelfiend with exaggerated understanding, "I see you do not care for Orlov's speciality. I cannot permit my honoured guest to go without his meal, so I will get Orlov to prepare something of your own choice."

"It really doesn't matter," Rupert said quickly.

"Then enjoy a glass of wine while I eat," he suggested.

"Er, yes. A glass of wine would be most welcome."

Orlov poured out a glass of vintage red wine, and while Rupert drank, his father tucked into his Goat's Head Surprise.

"Merely to dampen my curiosity," the vampire said between mouthfuls, "please tell me how you

49

and your friends propose to get rid of me this time?"

Rupert spluttered, and his wine ran down his chin and on to his shirt. "I, er, don't know what you're talking about," he stammered, but he had never been a very good liar.

"No games are necessary, my dear boy," said Krinkelfiend. "I know all about your plans. I have eyes everywhere. I could have dealt with you at any time. You know that. Indeed, it is only because of your vampire blood that I have permitted us this opportunity to talk. Otherwise I would have had my associates from the graveyard turn you into one of them."

Rupert gulped at the thought. "And what do you intend to do with me after this evening?" he asked nervously.

"A good question, my meddling guest. A good question indeed," replied Krinkelfiend. "But let us not talk of violence while we are enjoying such a tranquil evening, and Orlov's exquisite Goat's Head Surprise."

Krinkelfiend raised his glass at Rupert. "To the

good times of yesteryear, and the good times yet to come."

Rupert raised his glass and took a worried sip, wondering just what was to become of him.

Orlov quickly pulled a lever on the wall. A large net fell from the ceiling, completely trapping them.

◀ Chapter Four
Into the Lion's Den

By mid-morning the following day, Rupert hadn't returned, and Inspector Klaw and Professor von Morcumstein decided it was time to act. Both agreed that a visit to the castle should be first on their list. Both agreed it should be safe enough to go in daylight.

Then the professor had a thought.

"Helsing!" he suddenly said. "We should visit

Helsing first. He said he would keep in contact with us, but there is nothing to prevent *us* keeping in contact with *him*."

"To what end?" asked Klaw.

"He has lived all his life here in Bran, my dear Inspector. What is the betting he knows the castle better than anyone else?"

"Other than the vampire currently occupying it," pointed out the inspector.

"Maybe so, but it is a start," said the professor, rubbing his hands excitedly. "I do so hope I have the chance to see this dagger close up."

"Very well," nodded Klaw. "We will go and visit him."

"But where will we find him, Inspector?" asked the professor. "Helsing doesn't go to the cathedral until the evening."

"I wasn't thinking of the cathedral," said Klaw mysteriously.

At noon, Inspector Klaw and Professor von Morcumstein entered the third of Bran's three inns, and this time they were not disappointed. "There is

Helsing, in the corner," nodded the professor. "You were right to assume he would be in one of these drinking houses."

Helsing wasn't surprised to see them again, but he was immediately concerned by the absence of Rupert. "Where is he?" he asked.

Klaw looked to the professor who looked back at Helsing. "Rupert is missing," explained the professor. "He went to the castle last night, and hasn't returned. Of course, he might be on to something and therefore unable to return just yet. . ."

"This is most unfortunate," said Helsing, as if he were talking about nothing more than a bad cold. "Not only for Rupert, but for all mankind. Rupert, as you will know, is only half-vampire. But I had hoped he might have enough power within him to control his father." Helsing shrugged. "A silly idea really, especially as Krinkelfiend holds the dagger."

"I don't think we should worry ourselves too much just yet," said the professor. "Despite appearances, Krinkelfiend is rather fond of his son. He is all he has left."

"He has Dracula," said Helsing. "He needs no more."

"Couldn't we try a mass attack on the castle?" suggested Inspector Klaw. "You know. Get all the local forces together and explain the situation."

"To go blundering in with an army would just bring about a quicker and larger demise of our people," Helsing said.

"What, then?" said Klaw.

"We must fight fire with fire," said Helsing.

"Garlic and the crucifix?" said the professor excitely.

"It is a fact that vampires are repelled by these things you mention, Professor," admitted Helsing. "They could at least assist us in gaining access to our young friend and create the necessary time to spirit him away from the place." Helsing sighed deeply.

"I once knew Arnold Krinkelfiend well," he told them. "I know how his mind works. His mind is a little deranged, but he is an intelligent man. He plans carefully. And, right now, he believes he has acquired some magical access to Dracula:

he also knows that he has remarkable powers of his own. He is under no pressure to do anything. He can control the situation at his own pace. We can be grateful for that as it will give us a little more time to think and to act."

"Perhaps," mused the professor, "he will want to show off his son to Dracula. Perhaps he even dreams of convincing him to rejoin the dark side."

"Then let's hope he fails," said Klaw, "or it really is curtains for everyone."

"Oh, he'll fail all right," Helsing assured them. "I spent much time with Rupert when he was a young lad. I encouraged him to find his true self. I never told him what I thought of his father or his father's beliefs, but I encouraged him to make a decision."

"Be a man or be a vampire, you mean?" said Klaw.

"Exactly that. However," said Helsing, "if our learned friend the professor is correct, and Krinkelfiend is still fond of his son, then we have more time than I had dared to hope. But if your next step is to visit the castle, you must go alone. I am too old. I will slow you down. It is best I observe at a distance."

"As you wish," said the professor (who was no youngster himself). "Shall we agree to meet back here tomorrow at the same time with any news of what we might have discovered?"

"An excellent proposal, Professor von Morcumstein," said Helsing with a gentle smile.

🦇 🦇 🦇

"You would think," began Inspector Klaw, as he and the professor climbed towards Bran Castle that afternoon, "you would be able to get hold of a small bit of garlic and a crucifix in a town with vampire history."

"Yes. Most unfortunate," said the professor. "There isn't a garlic delivery due for another two days thanks to some festival which has procured masses of the stuff."

"And the crucifixes," added Klaw, "are only sold from one shop which only the other night burned down in mysterious circumstances."

"What a coincidence!" said the professor, not for

a moment believing it to be so. "I think our Krinkelfiend vampire is preparing a safe path for his master's arrival."

"Whatever, it means we are to enter the castle totally unarmed," said Klaw. "Not a refreshing thought. But at least it is daytime. Vampires sleep during the day."

The professor chuckled loudly. "You are becoming quite an expert on vampire behaviour, Inspector."

"Hardly that," smiled Klaw, before adding, more worriedly, "but I do wish our friend Helsing had accompanied us. He seems to think he can do more if he stays on the outside of our little group."

"Perhaps he can," said the professor. "Whatever, I feel sure there is more to Herr Helsing than meets the eye."

"How do you mean?" asked Klaw.

"Oh, I don't know," said the professor mysteriously. "I just sense that he is more interested in Dracula's return than in any acts of mischief currently being created by Count Krinkelfiend.

I might be wrong, of course. There is much in the air to confuse us all at present."

"Anything to do with vampires tends to leave me confused," said Klaw with feeling.

A short while later, they were standing at an entrance to the Castle. The arched wooden doorway creaked agonizingly on ancient hinges as the two men forced their way into the main courtyard.

"Somewhat eerie," said the professor with a grin. "Just how I like it."

"I was happier at the hotel," complained Klaw.

"Then you are not going to like my next suggestion," said the professor. "You see, if I were a vampire fearful of enemies and daylight, I think I should not feel very safe if I rested *above* ground."

"If you're suggesting that we go underground, then you're right," said Klaw. "I *don't* like your suggestion." He thought for a moment before reluctantly saying, "But I suppose you do have a very good point."

The professor began searching around the courtyard. "If you could tell me what we're looking for, Professor?" said Klaw.

"I was hoping that there might be... Ah, yes. Over here, Inspector."

"A trap door in the ground," said Klaw, moving to the professor's side.

"Exactly! A way beneath the castle, perhaps. Then we can search for Krinkelfiend. A stake through the heart is our only real hope of dealing with him."

"We have no stake," Klaw pointed out.

"I'm sure we'll find something we can sharpen to a point which will suffice. And with Krinkelfiend dealt with, we can concentrate on rescuing our poor friend."

Klaw shook his head. "How do we always manage to get into these dreadful situations?" he asked.

"It's all in the name of good," chuckled the professor. "You can guarantee that tonight Krinkelfiend will have even more of his Undead associates materializing to wreak havoc on the town."

The professor walked a few steps closer to the trap door.

"Let's discover what we shall discover," he said, heaving back the trap door. Klaw rushed to assist him.

They climbed down the steps into the tunnel just as Rupert had the night before. But unlike Rupert they required some light, so Inspector Klaw struck a match.

"Footprints!"

The professor bent over to get a better look. "Yes. And lots of them coming to and fro." He straightened his back. "I think we can assume we are heading in the right direction."

"I was afraid you were going to say that," whispered Klaw.

As Rupert had discovered, they found that the tunnel wound on and on as if there was to be no end to it.

A while later though, they came to a door. Klaw stopped to examine the ground more closely. "More footprints, but these are scattered, suggesting a struggle of some kind," whispered Klaw. "I wonder if one set belongs to Rupert!"

"Possibly," said the professor. "Let's see if we cannot discover more intriguing signs of visitors."

He opened the door and a few moments later they were standing in the crypt. A pool of light from a single flaming torch illuminated the cold stone floor.

"What a delightful place," whispered Klaw sarcastically.

"Yes. Not the most cheerful room I've ever been in," agreed the professor. "But ideal for concealing oneself during the deadly daylight hours."

"You think ... you think Krinkelfiend is here now?" whispered Klaw.

"I've no idea," shrugged the professor, who was already excitedly studying various bits and pieces with his usual curiosity.

"For you, this is like a child being allowed to roam freely in a toyshop," remarked Klaw.

"Oh yes," said the professor, distractedly. "Quite so. A good analogy, Inspector. I do find the whole adventure most satisfying."

"It was the same when we were trapped in King Konstantine's Palace," said Klaw. "You were more interested in holding a conversation with Count Krinkelfiend than worrying about how we were going to escape."

"Escape?" said a shrill voice. "There *is* no escape!"

Both men looked across the crypt towards where the voice had come from. There, standing beneath the flickering orange and red light of a burning torch was the most hideous looking man either of them had ever seen.

"Stay where you are!" ordered the strange man.

"He appears to be alone," whispered Klaw to the professor.

"And stop whispering."

"I fancy we can deal with this one."

"I said stop whispering! It's rude to whisper. Don't say I haven't warned you!"

"I'm most sorry," bowed the professor. "We were just wondering who you are!"

"I'm... Hang on. *I'm* supposed to ask who *you* are."

Inspector Klaw made steps towards him. "We have come to find a friend of ours. His name is Rupert. Perhaps you've heard of him?"

"I've heard of lots of people," said Orlov prodding his chest. "I bet I've heard of lots more people than you've heard of."

"The man is a fool," whispered Klaw.

"I heard that!" said Orlov.

"What shall we do with him, Professor?"

"Tell me, er. . ." the professor began.

"Orlov!" said Orlov. "That's not my real name, though. My real name's Volro."

Inspector Klaw scratched his head. "But that's Orlov spelled backwards."

"Yes," smiled Orlov. "Though 'Orlov' could be 'Volro' spelled backwards. All depends how you look at it. Clever, eh? My poor mum, who I never met, must have been very clever."

The professor gently waved his hand. "We just wish to find our friend, Rupert, then we will leave you in peace."

"Rupert," said Orlov, thinking a moment. "I've got it!" he said, clapping his hands.

Klaw smiled. At last they were getting somewhere with this fool. "Rupert," said Orlov, "is ... Trepur!"

"What?" said Klaw.

The professor sighed.

"Rupert," said Orlov, shrugging his one working shoulder. "If you spell Rupert backwards, it spells Trepur! Give me another one. This is fun, is this."

"Come, Inspector," said the professor. "I think we must progress alone."

As they turned to leave the crypt, Orlov quickly pulled a lever on the wall. A large net fell from the ceiling, completely trapping them.

"What's happening?" cried Klaw.

"I think we've been outsmarted," said the professor.

"By ... by *him*!" said Klaw.

"Sorry," said Orlov. "Can't let you go without letting my master know you're here. We have rules, you know. This isn't any old castle."

Orlov limped from the room, and the professor and Inspector Klaw stopped struggling. There was no escaping the net.

"Our only real hope," said the professor to his friend, "is that Rupert can manage to do something."

"That's true," said Klaw, brightening. "He must have guessed we would come to the castle to look for him."

At that very moment, Rupert was, in fact, doing very little. Accepting it was pointless to attempt to escape his powerful father, Rupert had allowed himself to be chained to a wall in one of the many dungeons Dracula had had installed. But he remained optimistic.

"Maybe the professor and the Inspector can manage to do something. Indeed, they might be arranging a daring rescue at this very moment..."

Helsing had not held out too much hope for Inspector Klaw and the professor's plan to visit the castle, even if they intended making their call during the relative safety of daylight.

Early that evening, following his lunchtime rendezvous with Klaw and the professor, Helsing made a move of his own.

Helsing led a six-man workforce through the graveyard carrying shovels on their shoulders as soldiers might carry rifles. They thought it rather odd that the old man wanted them to dig a large hole at one corner of the graveyard where it ran

67

into the fields and woods beyond. No one was going to see the flowers at their best if they were planted out of sight. But he was paying them a good fee for the work, so who were they to complain?

Helsing's biggest problem had been clearing his idea with the Bishop at the cathedral. He felt guilty that he'd told him a white lie – that he wanted to plant new flower beds – but it was a lie which was for the best possible cause. And with Rupert and his friends seemingly held prisoner at the castle, he had to do something to help upset the vampire's plans.

"How deep do you want us to dig this hole?" asked one of the men taking off his jacket.

"Fifteen to twenty feet should do," replied Helsing.

"How much?" gasped the man, and his fellow workers exchanged worried looks.

"Only if there's enough daylight," said Helsing.

"You must be planning on planting very large flowers," said the worker.

Helsing smiled weakly and gave a tiny shrug.

He could hardly explain that he was laying a trap for the Undead.

"*My dear former son... I trust you slept well? So sorry to keep you hanging around like this.*"

☙ Chapter Five
Guests of a Vampire

At midnight, Count Krinkelfiend opened the large door to the dungeon. "My dear former son," he said grandly as he swept into the grim, dank room. "I trust you slept well? So sorry to keep you hanging around like this."

"Not the best sleep I've ever had," said Rupert. "When I did eventually fall asleep, I was quickly awoken by voices."

"Ah yes – voices," said the vampire. "Friends of yours, actually, who just happened to drop in. What a cosy household we are becoming."

Rupert's heart sank. If the professor and the inspector were now prisoners too, then there was no way out of this mess.

"I expect you would like to see them?" said the vampire.

Rupert gave a single tired nod and said, "Yes. I would like that very much."

With that, Krinkelfiend clicked his fingers and the chains which had held Rupert to the wall cracked open. "Follow me," he ordered.

They marched at a brisk pace down neglected corridors. Rupert was impressed that his father seemed to know every twist and turn in the ancient building.

A downward stairwell led them to another cell. Krinkelfiend clicked his fingers again and the door opened for him. "The trouble with having such wonderful powers," he explained to his son smugly, "is that one grows increasingly lazy when it comes to doing something simple like opening a door."

"So I can imagine," said Rupert, knowing how feeble his own powers were in comparison.

"It is a shame you have no powers of your own," said Krinkelfiend, guessing what his son was thinking.

"Who said I've lost my powers?" said Rupert, trying not to act as though he was truly offended.

"It wasn't hard to work out," said his father. "You were always an impetuous boy, so you wouldn't have waited around Bran Castle once you were trapped. You would have done all in your power to escape. I recall you turned into a bat when we were at Viktoria Palace. And you had learned the art of cloaking, no less. On that particular occasion you became a chair, I believe."

There was nothing for Rupert to say. The count knew too much. It was true that he had learned to cloak – to take on the form of any object. But that power, like all his powers, had seemingly deserted him. Even the simple chain-breaking spell he had tried only moments before his father had stepped into the dungeon and used the same spell so easily, had failed miserably. His human lifestyle had dulled his magical skills. He followed his father meekly into the cell.

Inside, Orlov was examining his hideous face in a mirror. He quickly hid the mirror when he heard Count Krinkelfiend approach. Rupert looked up. Professor von Morcumstein and Inspector Klaw were hanging in a steel net like a rare species preparing to be transported to a museum.

"You are keeping our guests entertained, Orlov?" remarked Krinkelfiend.

"Er, yes, Count," said Orlov, relieved he hadn't noticed the mirror.

"Professor! Inspector! Are you all right?" asked Rupert.

"In a manner of speaking," replied the professor.

"I'm so sorry about all this," said Rupert.

"Not your fault," said Inspector Klaw, reassuringly.

"This is all most touching," sneered Krinkelfiend. "It brings a lump to my throat. Ah, Professor von Morcumstein. How good it is to see you again," said Krinkelfiend with a bow. "I did so enjoy our last discussion. For a mortal you are most enlightened on vampirism."

"Thank you," said the professor, genuinely pleased by the flattery.

"You will be glad to know – *all* of you will be glad to know – that we will have longer to spend in conversation on this occasion."

"You intend keeping us alive?" said an incredulous Rupert.

"I think your father wouldn't want us to forgo the opportunity of meeting Vlad Dracula," explained the professor.

"Again, I find you one step ahead of me, Herr Professor," congratulated the vampire. "Our lord and master will indeed soon be summoned," he went on, suddenly more serious than before. "The time when he will return to rule this planet is almost with us. We shall all be his slaves."

"And you're happy to be a slave of Vlad Tepes?" asked Rupert.

"I, myself, intend to be his right-hand man, as it were. After all," said Krinkelfiend, "it is through me and my hard work that he has the opportunity to return. If it hadn't been for my understanding of the dagger and its powers, it would probably still be sitting at Viktoria Palace, stuck on a wall and serving no more than a decorative purpose."

In the ensuing short silence, Krinkelfiend made a sudden decision. He clicked his fingers and the net lowered to the ground.

"Orlov," he ordered. "Take our guests to the guest quarters. I wouldn't want them to think we were uncivilized. It is, after all, very cold and miserable down here, and I'm reliably informed that mortal flesh reacts badly to such conditions."

"Very good, Count," said Orlov, hobbling to the open door. The three bemused men followed him.

Of all the things Count Arnold Krinkelfiend was, thought Inspector Klaw, predictable wasn't one of them.

"We will meet again later, gentlemen," said Krinkelfiend. "In the meantime, I have important matters to attend to. I'm sure you understand."

Just to be safe, Krinkelfiend had the professor, Inspector Klaw and Rupert locked in separate rooms. Though Krinkelfiend was more than positive there wasn't a chance of them escaping, he didn't want to give them the opportunity to make a plan. Their working together as a team in Gertcha had cost him dearly; he had no intention of making that mistake again.

He would have got rid of them at once had it not been so close to the arrival of his lord and master. He felt the professor deserved the opportunity to meet Dracula before departing this life, and somehow he hoped that his son might change his ways, once in the presence of the great vampire.

"For the time being, it's better they stew alone," he thought, rubbing his hands and thinking how diabolically clever he had grown during his time entombed in the dagger.

Thinking of the dagger made him rush to one of the large rooms which stood on the perimeter of the castle.

Making straight for a particular panel on a mahogany wall, he pressed the palm of his right hand against it. The panel sank back to reveal a small, secret cubbyhole. Inside was Dracula's dagger, which he now delicately withdrew from its sheath. Despite the lightless room, the jewels still sparkled, their glow making the count's eyes appear very red and fierce.

"Tonight!" he whispered to the dagger. "Tonight I will open the door between the past and the present."

He was just replacing the dagger as Orlov entered the room, but not so swiftly that Orlov didn't notice it. "I wish you wouldn't sneak up on me like that, Orlov," he said.

"Sorry, Master. It's these soft-soled shoes," he explained. "No one ever hears me. When I worked for our master, I didn't have such comfy soft-soled shoes. In fact, I didn't have any shoes at all, come to think of it."

"Yes, yes. Well, what is it, Orlov?"

"It's about the prisoners," said Orlov.

"*Guests*, Orlov, *guests*," the count corrected mildly.

"Oh yes. Well – it's about the guests, Count. Should I take them some food or is your plan to starve them?"

"Where is your sense of hospitality, Orlov?" chuckled Krinkelfiend. "Give them food, but do make sure it is something we would consider revolting. Their taste-buds are most unusual. Personally, I don't know how they stomach half the stuff they consume." He smiled widely. "Give me a good goat's head every time!"

"Oh yes, yes," said Orlov vaguely, busy thinking what a clever place the count had found to hide such a beautiful dagger. He knew about the dagger from his master, Dracula. If it was as powerful as he had been led to believe, perhaps his hideous face and deformed body could be transformed into something beautiful. The mirror he had come across earlier had reminded him just how hideous he looked.

"Leave me now, Orlov," ordered Krinkelfiend. "I need to prepare my mind for tonight's ceremony. It is the most important moment of my life."

"Very well, Count," said Orlov with an awkward bow. Then he spun around and shuffled from the room.

Orlov could see that the world beyond the castle had changed so much: did he really want to spend the rest of his years saying, "Yessir, nosir, three-bags-fullsir," to two vampires dressed like waiters? And he wondered what life was going to be like once his lord and master returned to the castle that evening. He had been so excited about it all. But now he was beginning to have doubts.

The dead forms began toppling into the hole like falling skittles.

🦇 Chapter Six

Orlov Begins to See Things Clearly

Helsing's trap for the Undead was complete. Now he was snuggled under a blanket against the darkest corner of the cathedral, which fortunately afforded him a perfect view of the fields and woods beyond the graveyard.

It was past eleven o'clock when the now familiar grating sound first echoed around him. He felt his pulse quicken.

The slabs of stone shifted. A moment later, the Undead's decomposing hands gripped the edges of their burial chambers and heaved themselves upright. Helsing was transfixed by this ghastly performance. Never in his long life had he seen – or expected to see – such a horrific sight.

The Undead figures seemed oblivious of each other – and, fortunately, of Helsing – as they traipsed like sleepwalkers towards the path leading to the fields. The fields, in turn, led to the castle. "I hope the hole is deep enough," Helsing said over and over again to himself.

In the dark, it was impossible to notice that the hole was covered by a green carpet. Even Helsing, who obviously knew it was there, was unable to say exactly where it began and where it ended. The dead forms, who began toppling into the hole like falling skittles, had no idea at all.

When the last one had disappeared, Helsing struggled to his stiff legs and hobbled across excitedly. He hardly dared peep over the precipice where the carpet and bodies had fallen. Taking a deep breath, he craned his neck forward. There they all were – some fifty of them – standing still like a collection of statues. Unable to proceed, they had merely shut down until given further instructions. "Slaves!" muttered Helsing. "You're nothing more than Krinkelfiend's slaves."

Helsing was pleased – more than pleased, delighted – with his night's work. Now he had solid proof of what was going on in his home town, he could summon help. But whose help? He had no idea who could be trusted in Bran. Not the authorities. Krinkelfiend was bound to have gathered agents for his own ends. It was a dilemma.

Meanwhile, on what was supposed to be his big night, Count Arnold Krinkelfiend was pacing the floor of his secret chamber, awaiting his army of Undead. Holding Dracula's dagger with a loving fondness, he asked his servant moodily, "What time now, Orlov?"

"Nearly midnight, Count."

"What keeps my children of the night, tonight of all nights?" After a further few minutes had passed, he said, "Orlov. Go to the cathedral and discover

what has happened. I have one of my strange feelings coming over me. I can sense outside
interference. But from whom? My three biggest
enemies are safely locked up here in the castle."

"The cathedral? Very good, Count," said Orlov,
watching Krinkelfiend return the dagger to a pocket
within his black cloak.

Standing at the edge of the deep hole in the cathedral's graveyard, Orlov soon discovered what had
become of Krinkelfiend's growing army. He was
about to turn and hobble as quickly as he could
back to the castle with the news, when something
inside his dull head signalled that this was an
important moment in his life – a turning point, one
might say. If someone had been clever enough to
lay this trap and spoil the count's evening, he rea-
soned, then surely he, Orlov, could be clever
enough to get hold of the dagger and try to secure
a little bit of power for himself? He didn't want
much: he wasn't greedy. Just enough to make people stop ordering him to do this and that and cook
meals and clean clothes. And, of course, enough to

straighten his leg, his back, his head; rearrange his fingers and toes so they were numerically perfect, and make him as handsome as a prince. "No," he decided, chuckling to himself. "That last one's asking a bit much."

Helsing had decided it was his duty to remain near his trap for the duration of the night. He didn't want someone having an accident. Even if falling down the hole didn't kill them, the sight of some fifty Undead bodies standing around would surely do the trick. There was nothing for it but to stay and guard his terrible secret until daybreak.

He had seen a figure arrive: seen this deformed creature hobble confidently up to the hole, turn around, stop, scratch his head, chuckle then move quickly and silently into the darkness. Helsing was confused. It wasn't the behaviour he would have expected from a resident of the town. It took him a few moments to realize what was amiss.

"Of course," he said aloud. "He came into the graveyard expecting to find something. He must be from the castle." He strained his ageing eyes to examine the figure. "It can't be?" he muttered. "But surely it is Orlov I see before me. And not a day older to look at than he was all those hundreds of years ago." Helsing had a clear memory of Orlov hovering around the castle performing errands for Vlad Dracula. "He must now be working for Krinkelfiend."

Helsing spent what was left of the night planning a way he could use Orlov to his own advantage.

"Who is it who dares meddle in this fashion?" growled Krinkelfiend when Orlov returned with his disappointing report.

"Can't be anything to do with your prison— um, guests," Orlov corrected swiftly. "We've got them here."

"Then it is either someone who knows them," mused the vampire, "or someone who knows *me*. But who? I haven't been in these parts for some years. Who could possibly know I have returned?"

"I could find out for you," said Orlov. "I'm not a complete fool!"

"Why, what part is missing?" sneered Krinkelfiend. "However," he went on, when Orlov didn't show any sign of appreciating his little joke, "you could be of some use. You are safe to act in daylight hours as well as at night. But you must not draw attention to yourself. Be like the shadow you are when you drift around this castle. Don't be heard or seen."

"I'm good at that sort of thing," smiled Orlov lop-sidedly.

"Meanwhile," said Krinkelfiend, "now that the ceremony has been delayed due to unforeseen circumstances, I will take a short bat-flight around the town." His face grew dark and threatening. "Woe betide the one who has stood in my way this night. I do not take kindly to people meddling with my plans. I shall delight in dealing with him personally."

Orlov swallowed hard and tried not to think too much about his plan to borrow the dagger.

*At that moment, one of the window panes exploded
and a bat flew into the room.*

⚜ Chapter Seven
Rupert, and a Happy Discovery

Having made the suggestion that he should go and find out who was meddling in the count's affairs, Orlov wasn't quite so sure where to begin. If he couldn't be seen or heard, who could he speak to and where could he visit, he wondered, as he walked guardedly through the dark night-time streets of Bran.

"I'd have been better off staying at the castle and borrowing the dagger," he grumbled.

What Orlov didn't – couldn't – have realized was that he was more the hunted than the hunter. Helsing had been spying on the castle at a safe distance since two in the morning and had seen Orlov leave just before three o'clock. It had meant neglecting the pit in the graveyard, but this was more important. Besides, he was confident that the Undead weren't going anywhere, and if anyone was silly enough to fall into it between now and daybreak ... well, they should have been in bed, like most honest people. The thought of bed made Helsing yawn. He was far too old for this sort of caper.

He was about to make his move when the gentle sound of fluttering wings drifted above him. It was a bat. A *large* bat. Suddenly, in a burst of purple smoke, the bat landed on the street next to Orlov and changed into Krinkelfiend. Orlov jumped in fright, then realized it was only the count making one of his dramatic appearances. Helsing shrank back into the shadows.

"How goes your investigation, Orlov?" said Krinkelfiend.

"A little slow, Count," said Orlov, as his heart began to resume its regular beat. "I saw someone pushing a vegetable barrow towards the market place. The day starts early for those who work at the market."

"Most interesting," said Krinkelfiend in a way that suggested it wasn't interesting at all. "The activities of the inhabitants of Bran are not of particular importance to me right now, Orlov. Just find the one who is meddling in my plans."

"I'll get there in the end, Count," promised Orlov. "You can count on me. Oh, sorry about that. Didn't mean to make a joke."

The count frowned. He didn't appreciate jokes unless he made them himself. He wondered to himself how the mighty Dracula could have put up with such a deformed fool as Orlov.

"I'm going to inspect the Undead," sighed Krinkelfiend. "Move carefully, Orlov."

Another puff of purple smoke, and the bat was soon swooping over distant rooftops.

"I must be careful," Helsing told himself. "It seems Krinkelfiend is not afraid of snooping around the town."

Helsing tied a loop in the rope he was carrying, and moved stealthily – or as stealthily as a man of his years could move – towards Orlov. At the last moment, just as Orlov realized someone was behind him, he tossed the loop over his head like a makeshift lasso, and tugged his prisoner towards him.

"What's going on?" squawked Orlov – the last words he said before Helsing banged him on the head with a heavy stick.

"That should keep you quiet," he said, and dragged his prisoner towards his tiny house, which wasn't very far from where they had been standing.

Rupert paced up and down in the large, unfurnished bedroom where his father had confined him. The walls were solid stone, pitted and crumbly in parts, and the door to the room was solid oak. The moon shone in through a small barred window making shadow-lines across the dusty floor. The warm night air wafted in between the bars, whispering all around him.

"I have to get out," Rupert kept telling himself.

"Father's being really quite impossible this time. He must be stopped before he awakes Dracula." He looked desolately at the solid door and the surprisingly strong iron bars across the window. "It's utterly hopeless."

He stopped pacing as a thought came to him. "Utterly hopeless for a mortal," he said aloud, "but what about for a man who was – perhaps still is – half vampire?"

He stood before the window. "I command you to disappear," he told the bars, which did nothing of the sort. He turned away. "A poor start," he said.

Next, he moved towards the door. "I command you to unlock yourself and open," he ordered sternly. A few miserable sparks sizzled at the end of his fingertips, but the door stared back blankly. "Well, that wasn't much use," he said glumly. "There was a time," he went on, moving back towards the barred window, "when all I had to do was snap my fingers like this..." he snapped his fingers – "and my every wish would be obeyed."

He stared out upon the moonlit landscape feeling

quite defeated – until he realized that the bars were no longer there.

He glanced at his hands and smiled. "My powers!" he gasped. "They *are* returning. Being amongst other vampires, and in the very home of Dracula, must be helping. The whole thing is in the mind. I must make my mind focus on each task. I must *think* like a vampire."

Feeling much more confident, he had a thought and snapped his fingers again. A bowl of lush red apples appeared at his feet. "Marvellous!" he exclaimed, bending down and picking out the juiciest one. "I was feeling a bit peckish."

He had another thought – a big thought which would be the final proof that his powers were returning fully – and snapped his fingers. A puff of purple smoke filled the room and a small bat appeared in Rupert's place. It let out a triumphant squeak and shot out of the window.

The professor, who was leaning against his his recent meeting with Krinkelfiend, was suddenly distracted by something outside his window. "How odd!" he remarked. "A bat coming towards me with what looks like an apple in its mouth."

Rupert flew in between the bars and, in a puff of purple smoke, became human again.

"Good evening, Professor," said Rupert, spitting the apple out of his mouth. "Guess what?"

"You have rediscovered your powers?" said the professor.

"Exactly!"

"This is truly wonderful, young man," said the professor, clapping his hands. "Perhaps now we really can prevent your father bringing Dracula back among us."

"That will take some doing," said Rupert, "but it is a start in the right direction."

"What is your next move?" asked the professor.

"I'll tell the inspector the good news, then I'm going to visit Helsing to see if he knows of any outside developments. I'll be back before dawn."

"I'm not planning on going anywhere, young man," said the professor, and before he had finished speaking, Rupert was a bat again and flying away between the bars of his window.

"Well, my dear Orlov," smiled Helsing. "I had no idea we would meet again after all these centuries. How did Dracula manage it? He must have frozen you, I imagine."

"You won't get anything out of me, Helsing," snorted Orlov, who was tied to the bannister rail in Helsing's house.

"I've told you," said Helsing, "I'm not interested in receiving any in-depth information on life at Castle Bran. All I wish to know is that my friends are safe, and what Krinkelfiend is up to. Come, Orlov. You are one of very few who have known the real me. We can trust each other."

"I only cook the meals, polish the shoes, deal with all the mundane twaddle," said Orlov. "You're speaking to the wrong man."

"I doubt that, somehow," said Helsing, lowering himself into a comfy chair near the staircase.

"You'll have to let me go sooner or later," said Orlov, "or the count will come looking for me, and then what are you going to do?"

"So, you do know quite a bit about Count Arnold Krinkelfiend, then?"

"I didn't say that," said Orlov, shaking his uneven head.

"Yet you can predict his moods and reactions," said Helsing. "I find that very suggestive, in terms of your relationship."

"Stop waffling and let me go, you silly old fool!"

"Sticks and stones, my dear friend; sticks and stones."

At that moment, one of the window panes exploded and a bat flew into the room.

"Ha!" laughed Orlov. "Looks like you're in big trouble sooner than I'd expected, old timer."

Helsing froze in his seat, but to his delight and amazement, from a vast puff of purple smoke emerged Krinkelfiend. Not vampire Arnold Krinkelfiend, but Krinkelfiend Junior.

"Rupert, my boy," gasped Helsing.

"Hello, Helsing," said Rupert, clasping the old man's hand then turning to see Orlov attached to the bannister rail. "Do these come with all Transylvanian properties?"

"Oh yes," smiled Helsing. "No decent house is without one."

"You two can scoff," said Orlov, screwing up his face, "but just wait till your father comes after you."

"Fortunately, my misguided father is unaware of my departure from the castle."

"But for how long, eh?"

"He is right," said Helsing, all at once concerned. "It's only a matter of time before he tracks us down."

Rupert turned to Orlov again. "Where does he keep the dagger?" he demanded.

"What dagger?" grinned Orlov.

"You know what dagger," said Rupert. "You, who shuffle around the castle acting all innocent."

"It's no good, Rupert," said Helsing. "He serves only one master."

"One master at present," said Rupert, "but soon *two* masters; isn't that right, Orlov? Oh yes, I've seen your expression each time Father says 'Do this, Orlov, do that, Orlov'. I can see behind your furtive wide eyes, Orlov."

Orlov didn't reply, but Rupert could tell he was on the right track. "Two masters ordering you about the castle while they plan the destruction of mankind," Rupert went on. "What will become of poor Orlov, then? With all the Undead as slaves, who will need the limping, ugly Orlov to tend their needs?"

"I... I... They will still need me," stammered Orlov.

"I don't think so," hummed Rupert. "And I don't think you really wish to remain a servant for the rest of your days, do you? Of course, the dagger could take care of all that. If I had the dagger it could be used to make you pretty again – make you whole. Indeed, make you strong and handsome. A new life would await you if we had the dagger."

A large contented grin passed fleetingly over Orlov's face.

"Where is it, Orlov?" whispered Rupert. "Where is the beautiful bejewelled weapon that can bring you a happiness you have only ever been able to dream of until now?"

"He... He will punish me if I betray him," squeaked Orlov.

"What can be worse than the position you are already in?" said Helsing. "You are a deformed slave."

"Will you promise to use the dagger to make me wise and wonderful and beautiful and ... and..."

"Yes, yes," said Rupert. "I will do all in my powers to transform you into an intelligent, handsome man. You will look like ... like a prince, when I have finished with you."

"A prince?" sighed Orlov. "I like the sound of that."

"Free him, Helsing," said Rupert. Helsing began untying the bonds from Orlov's hands.

As he did so Orlov said, "He keeps it in the room he uses as a study. There's a false panel in the wooden wall."

"Then we must hurry there at once," said Rupert.

Arnold Krinkelfiend could see the sharp silhouette of Bran Castle as he swept through the night air at great speed. Soon it would be daybreak. He needed to hide himself. But there was just enough darkness left for him to take a quick look at his "guests", before retiring for the day.

He made a pass by the professor's window and saw the wise old man seated against a wall writing furiously in his notebook. Inspector Klaw was still pacing sullenly up and down. "He'll wear his shoes out," chuckled the flapping vampire.

He hovered a moment then landed on the window ledge of Rupert's room. He could see his former son stretched out asleep on the floor. "He's definitely becoming too human," he thought. "Fancy wanting to sleep during the night. Ugh!" And with that, Krinkelfiend swooped towards one of the cone-shaped turrets and entered the castle, at once transforming into human shape. The grey scratch on the distant horizon, which signalled the approaching dawn, meant it was time for bed.

Rupert opened first one eye then the other. "That was close," he told Helsing.

"Yes. *Too* close," said Helsing, moving out of the shadows of the room. "A good job our friend here had the keys for the doors and knows all the short cuts through the castle."

They both looked in the approximate direction of Orlov who, like Helsing, had been hiding in a dark corner of the room.

"I'm only helping on the understanding you steal the dagger and make me beautiful."

"Yes, yes, yes," said Rupert. "We've been through all that, Orlov. But first things first. Daylight is upon us and so Father will be sleeping. We must release the others, then find this secret place where Father keeps the dagger."

"I hope you know what you're doing," moaned Orlov. "If he finds out then we've had it."

"You want a pretty face, don't you?" said Rupert. "Now, come on. We must act fast so he doesn't find out." He looked upon the tired and drawn features of Helsing. "You stay here and catch up on some sleep," he told him. "You've done more than enough for one night."

"Do you know, I think you're right," said Helsing curling up in one corner of the room. "But I mustn't rest long," he yawned. "The Undead in the grave-yard must be attended to before someone discovers them. And I need to find someone in authority who is still trustworthy, so I can tell them what's been going on in Bran."

"I'll wake you in an hour or so," promised Rupert.

"It will still be very early in the day."

"Thank you. That is most kind."

In the time it took Orlov and Rupert to leave the room, Helsing was sound asleep.

*The very moment the blade made contact with the ruby,
a blue light shot up Rupert's arm and threw him backwards...*

☙ Chapter Eight
Helsing in Trouble

On freeing his friends, Rupert updated them on recent events, including the fact that Orlov was now on their side. After a hasty discussion, Inspector Klaw made straight for the graveyard to keep guard while Helsing was sleeping. Being a policeman, he'd have some authority in dealing with any enquiries. Meanwhile, the professor went with Orlov and Rupert in search of Dracula's dagger. None of them was quite sure what they would do with the dagger should they find it, other than keep it as far away from Count Krinkelfiend as possible.

Inspector Klaw was shocked to discover he wasn't the first arrival at the cemetery. As he made his way through the churchyard, he could see a group of very official-looking men. And they were gathered around the large hole that Helsing's team of workmen had dug.

A tall, stooping man with an angular, solemn face – the sort of face that only smiled at someone's misfortune – appeared to be in charge. Inspector Klaw quickly introduced himself.

The man looked him up and down for a moment. "I am Sprantz, mayor of Bran. What do you know of this matter?"

Klaw was uncertain if he could trust him, but felt to do otherwise would make the mayor suspicious. He briefly tried to explain the situation, which was not easy to do.

"I see," said Sprantz when he had finished. "You say it was Helsing who said he'd set a trap for ... for the Undead?"

"That's right," smiled Klaw, patiently. "And that's why there, in the deep hole, you will find ... you will find..."

He didn't finish his sentence. Looking briefly in the hole he discovered there was nothing at all there to find save a pile of old rags and heaps of dust.

"Oh no!" sighed Klaw. "They've disintegrated. This is the vampires' way, you see. Once daylight strikes them, they turn to ash. I should have remembered. So should Helsing, for that matter."

The mayor and his three companions exchanged knowing looks. "I think we should pay Helsing a visit," said the mayor, his voice slow yet strangely menacing. "He is getting on in years and ... and not totally reliable these days. The moment has arrived, I feel, when we should consider giving him some help."

"Rimpton?" suggested one of the others.

"What's Rimpton?" asked Klaw.

"An asylum where they lock up the totally insane," said the same man.

"More a hospital with friendly, caring, staff," amended the mayor, through a tight, sickly grin.

"No. You don't understand," said Klaw. "There's

nothing wrong with Helsing. You can't lock him away with the insane."

"So, you believe his wild stories, too?" said the mayor, his white, bony face completely void of expression.

"I... I..." Klaw knew he had to be careful or he'd find himself in a similar straitjacket to the one they intended putting on poor Helsing. "I think he deserves the benefit of the doubt," he said, choosing his words with great care. "He's lived the whole of his life here in Bran, and has been a model citizen."

"He has a point," said one of the group.

"But we can't have him going around digging giant holes for Undead followers of ... vampires, was it?" checked the mayor.

"Yes. Well, Vlad Dracula, to be exact," said Klaw uncomfortably. "He once lived in the castle."

"Dracula died in the fifteenth century," said one of the others in the group. "If Helsing believes he's come back to life, then I'm beginning to come round to the idea of Rimpton."

"Perhaps I should just have a word or two with

Helsing," said the mayor kindly. "At least that would give us the chance for him to explain himself, and we can sort matters out after that."

Klaw thought a moment. The mayor seemed trustworthy enough. He clearly knew Helsing quite well.

"I'll let him know you want to talk to him," said Klaw. And made to leave the graveyard.

"Let's hurry up with this and get out," said Orlov, nervously.

"Calm yourself," said Rupert. "You know Father won't make an appearance during daylight."

"All the same, your father's got eyes in the back of his head. If he wore glasses, he would need two pairs!"

Rupert began pressing the panels with no success.

"More over here," said Orlov, pointing.

Rupert tried again where Orlov suggested, and a panel withdrew, revealing a small hollow containing the wonderful dagger and sheath.

"My, my," said the professor, excitedly.

Rupert felt an uneasy chill run through his veins,

as vivid images of the last time he had seen this glittering object came flooding back.

"*Now* what do we do?" asked Orlov.

"Keep your voice down," said Rupert.

"You were the one who said your father's not about."

"I know, but all the same..."

Rupert gently removed the dagger and pulled it from its sheath. After studying it for a short while, he handed it to the professor.

"Just look at it!" cried the professor, so overwhelmed he could hardly get his words out. "It is priceless. But what is it we are handling here, eh? I wouldn't begin to know how to tamper with its powers." He turned the dagger round and round in his long fingers. "I don't even know if that would be possible. The thing has proved to be very self-protective. It certainly won't allow us to destroy it. Indeed, it is likely that it is indestructible."

"So what should we do with it?" asked Rupert.

"Hide it," suggested Orlov. "That's after you've made me beautiful, like you promised."

"Yes, yes," said Rupert impatiently, for he in fact had not a clue as to how to go about instructing the dagger to perform such a feat.

"Whenever it does something," said the professor, "the power from it seems to emerge from the large Burmese ruby here. I would imagine that the ruby has an important role in the ceremony to return Vlad Dracula to mortal form."

"We could try to take the ruby out," said Rupert. "Perhaps, without the ruby, Dracula can *never* return."

"Is that wise?" asked the professor. "This dagger was not created to be tampered with. The ruby is possibly the key to the whole dagger. We do not know what we might unleash should we remove it."

"What else can we do if we don't try to disarm it?" said Rupert.

The professor thought a moment, then shrugged. "I was happy just to take it away from here, but... Oh, very well, young man. But be careful. We know from experience how powerful this dagger is."

Rupert produced a pocket knife and at once dug

the blade into the base of the ruby where it was set firmly. The very moment the blade made contact with the ruby, a blue light shot up Rupert's arm and threw him backwards on to the floor. The dagger fell noisily to the ground, spun in a circle for a few seconds then went still. For a moment no one dared move.

"It has a life of its own," whispered Orlov, awestruck.

The professor helped Rupert to his feet.

"I had wondered if it would protect itself," mused the professor.

"Shall I pick it up?" Rupert asked him.

"No harm in trying, I suppose," shrugged the professor. "Everything we try to do with this dagger is going to be a case of trial and error."

Rupert picked it up and smiled. "There. Nothing to it when you are, in part, a vampire." But as he spoke, his body started to shake, his skin turned pale and a strange, distant look filled his eyes.

"What is it? Are you ill?" asked the professor.

In reply, Rupert seemed to grow in stature, and

from somewhere deep inside him there came a voice that wasn't *his*.

The words spoken were, at first, in German, then Romanian. The message was clear: "Beware, those mortals who steal my vampire powers. My revenge shall be swift, as the revenge of Vlad Tepes always has been and for ever shall be."

The dagger zipped out of Rupert's hand, narrowly missed the professor's head and landed back in the cubbyhole, its sheath only a moment behind. The cubbyhole closed and Rupert fell to his knees coughing.

Orlov looked dumbfounded, while the professor rushed to help his young friend.

"I saw him," said Rupert. "I saw Vlad Tepes – Dracula. He is old – ancient – and covered in crawling maggots. A nightmare to behold."

"Nightmare is the right word for it," said the professor, "for what you most likely encountered was an image of Dracula's spirit entombed within the dagger. Should he return, he will, I imagine, do so in a more suitable form; one very much in keeping with people of today."

113

"If he doesn't, he'll certainly stand out in a crowd," said Rupert, trying to make light of his shock.

All three of them began looking towards the cubbyhole. "I think," said the professor, "we will have to forsake our plan to steal the dagger before something more alarming occurs. We must work on an alternative plan."

"You're right," said Rupert, and turning to Orlov, he added, "Sorry, but you'll have to wait a little longer for your beauty treatment!"

When Inspector Klaw was back inside the castle – after sneaking in through a secret door that Orlov had shown him – Helsing was awake and keen to hear his news. When Klaw reached the part about meeting Sprantz, Helsing frowned.

"This is going to be awkward," said Helsing. "Karl Sprantz is not to be trusted. He is as cunning as a fox, and cares for no one other than himself."

"He seemed very keen to have you put away at a place called Rimpton," said Klaw.

"I bet he did," sighed Helsing. "He doesn't care for me very much."

"What is this Rimpton place, exactly?" asked Inspector Klaw.

"Rimpton!" spat Helsing. "Rimpton is a badly run asylum – more a giant torture chamber. People taken there – and I mean taken, for no one goes there out of personal choice – never come out. It is a dark and cold place hidden in the forests behind Bran. People who in any way upset the general order of things, are placed there – permanently."

Klaw furrowed his brow. "Do you think the mayor knows something of Dracula and is deliberately trying to silence you?"

Helsing gave the question some thought. "That is possible, yes. It is more likely, however, that he wishes to avoid fear and disruption in the town rather than face the fact that we might have a problem on our hands. His three-year run as mayor is due to end next month. To stand a chance of re-election, he cannot afford mass panic."

"I see," said Klaw. "What we need to do then is make sure we avoid him at all costs."

"Quite right!" nodded Helsing. "Don't go back to the inn, for I would not put it past the unpleasant Sprantz to throw you into Rimpton just out of spite."

"Very well," said Klaw. Then he asked, "Do you think he knows Krinkelfiend?"

"It is a thought," nodded Helsing. "Perhaps Krinkelfiend is using the mayor for his own devices."

"We have enemies wherever we turn," remarked Klaw.

"Yes, we do. And always remember our mayor's name," advised Helsing. "It would be unwise to forget it."

At that moment, the professor, Rupert and Orlov came into the room.

"We've had a problem with the dagger," said Rupert, and with the help of the professor, he explained what they had been up to.

"I think we must get away from here before nightfall, with or without the dagger," said Helsing.

"I need to keep a watchful eye on our town mayor, Karl Sprantz, and you must find somewhere safe to hide while we work on a plan."

"So Sprantz," said Krinkelfiend, *"I am hoping you can cheer this weary vampire. What news?"*

♥ Chapter Nine
An Immortal One

Count Arnold Krinkelfiend was not a happy vampire. Last night, the delay in the ceremony to return his lord and master had more than ruffled him. And tonight he'd woken to find his meddling former son had found a way to escape from the castle: his former son, the idiotic policeman and the nosey Professor. And where was *Orlov*? What could have happened? Had Orlov gone off his ugly head and released them? If he had, then Orlov would die – very slowly.

"By morning I will have them in the palm of my hand," he cried, "and I will slowly crush the life out of them till they scream for mercy – which they won't get, of course."

Suddenly, he moved decisively towards a window, exploded into his bat form and took to the night air. He was on his way to question Sprantz. Perhaps the twisted mayor of Bran would have some useful information.

When the bat appeared on Sprantz's window and began tapping with its head, he went to let it in as though nothing were more normal.

"Good evening, Count," he said, with the hint of a bow.

The bat exploded in a puff of purple smoke. "So, Sprantz," said Krinkelfiend, brushing down his cloak with the back of a hand: "I am hoping you can cheer this weary vampire. What news?"

"My re-election is looking most favourable, and—"

"I meant news that would interest me," said the vampire, frowning.

"Oh yes, I've found out who's causing you trouble."

said Sprantz. "It is your old adversary, Helsing – the old fool succeeded in disposing of fifty of your followers last night."

"*Our* followers," corrected Krinkelfiend. "You are slowly becoming one of us, Sprantz. You bear the marks on your neck to prove it."

"Of course, Count," Sprantz said quickly. "Just a figure of speech."

"As for Helsing," spat Krinkelfiend, "I should have guessed it was his interference from the beginning. How could someone so intelligent and powerful as me have forgotten about him?"

"All is well on that score, Count," said Sprantz through a wicked smile. "I am making plans to have him taken to Rimpton … on a permanent basis. A one-way trip, you might say." Sprantz's evil smile revealed yellow, uneven teeth.

"I see," said Krinkelfiend, mulling this news over thoughtfully. "Then be careful," he warned. "Helsing is not what he seems."

"Surely we need not fear such an old man?" snorted Sprantz with contempt.

"Helsing knows things that even *I* do not know,"

admitted Krinkelfiend with some reluctance. "This isn't the first time he has come into conflict with our lord and master."

"He has met Dracula?" gasped Sprantz, astonished.

"On many occasions," confirmed Krinkelfiend nodding his head. "I'm no youngster myself," he went on, "but Helsing's first conflict with our lord and master came when both men were mortal – some two hundred years before my birth. Helsing was with an army of Turks. Both men were leaders of their units and fought long and hard. Dracula lost on that occasion."

Sprantz looked even more astonished. "But that would surely make him over … over…"

"Yes," said the vampire. "Helsing is well over four hundred and fifty years old."

"Then he is of vampire stock like you?" said Sprantz.

"No," said Krinkelfiend. "He is an Immortal One. He cannot die, but on the passing of every hundred years he turns into a young man and starts again. There are about twenty such men and women we know of with this unique gift, and they are greater enemies than any ordinary mortal, I assure you. Not only do they live for ever, but they have powers of resistance against vampirism. Their sole purpose is to rid the world of vampires."

"I see," nodded Sprantz, hurriedly pouring himself a glass of water. "If they live for ever, then they are forever there to challenge you."

"Precisely!" said Krinkelfiend. "Were I to destroy Helsing, which would be no simple matter, he would merely regenerate as a young man, and in a blink of the eye at that. But," he smiled, "we have yet to test the powers of the dagger against him. I am very hopeful that he will not be forever immortal once the dagger begins to reveal its strengths."

"And in the meantime?"

"Rimpton!" said Krinkelfiend. "Put him in Rimpton."

"As you wish," grinned Sprantz, rubbing his hands.

"By the time the night is out, there will be three, possibly four others to join him there."

"Even better," said Sprantz.

"But deal with Helsing first," said Krinkelfiend. "The others are less dangerous."

Krinkelfiend suddenly burst into a puff of purple smoke and turned into a bat. Flapping his wings, he left the room by the window through which he had come.

"Good morning, everyone," said Helsing. "Time to rise while the vampire sleeps."

"Oh no," sighed Orlov. "Tell me I'm dreaming. Tell me I haven't run away from Count Krinkelfiend, to find myself hiding in a crypt beneath the Bran Cathedral?"

"Indeed you have," said Helsing.

"Then tell me that we have the dagger."

"Indeed we do not," said Helsing.

"Oh, wonderful," cried Orlov. "Well, we've had it, then. He'll know by now that we've fled the castle. No more beautiful face for me. No more tall, elegant body to stride down the streets in. He'll probably turn me into something hideous, like a two-headed rat or a ... a mayor!"

"I know Father's powerful," said Rupert, "but let's not get carried away, eh Orlov?"

"You shouldn't have meddled with the ruby," said Orlov, turning angrily on Rupert.

"We had to try something," said the professor, raising a hand. "Taking the dagger was always going to be difficult, if not impossible."

"You must calm yourself, Orlov," said Helsing in a soothing tone. "The dagger belongs to no one, yet. Krinkelfiend is merely the carrier."

"Are you sure of this?" said the professor. "The power and ownership of the dagger are things we have discussed in the past without coming to any satisfactory conclusions."

"Oh yes," said Helsing. "I know much about our friend, Dracula. I even know about him from the time when he was as human as you, Professor." The professor leaned forward, fascinated. "His body was found in a snowy marsh near the island of Snagov, just north of Bucharest," said Helsing. "He was buried there, eventually. Whether he died in battle or was the victim of an assassin, no one knows for sure. It is something I must ask him if the opportunity arises. But as I say, that was a long, long time ago."

"You talk as someone who was actually present when all of this happened," remarked the professor.

"It... It is a subject which interests me, Professor," said Helsing. "Just as I know it interests you."

"That is very true, Herr Helsing."

"But how did he come to be a vampire?" asked Klaw,

who was finding Helsing's story quite fascinating.

"Because when he died he continued to exist," said Helsing.

"That was the answer Rupert gave me," said Klaw.

"It is the true answer," said Helsing. "His 'fatal' wounds healed themselves in less than the passing of a day. It was then he became aware he was no mere mortal. Then he found he could no longer eat or drink the foods and liquids required and appreciated by man, or bear the touch of daylight upon his skin. He became a creature of the night with increasing powers he couldn't comprehend, but slowly mastered."

"But how do *you* know so much?" pressed the professor, surprised by Helsing's knowledge.

"I, er, have studied much about Dracula and vampirism," he explained quickly. "You must remember that from your childhood, Rupert?" he said, turning for support from the young Krinkelfiend, who was familiar with Helsing's real past.

"I remember you knowing that my father was a vampire, and you telling me never to cross fully into the vampire world," recalled Rupert. "I think that's what made me find the mortal in myself when I most needed to."

"Excellent," smiled Helsing. "Then my time wasn't wasted."

"But what are we to do, gentlemen?" said Klaw, "We can't stay hiding in this crypt beneath the cathedral. Krinkelfiend adores places like this. He's sure to find us sooner or later."

"We're safe enough in daylight," said Helsing.

"And what do you propose we do for the rest of today?" asked Klaw, who was starting to miss his homeland, his apartment, and his simple way of life very much.

"Split up and roam the streets," suggested Helsing. "Let us see what the mood is like in Bran. By now we should have proved quite a thorn in Krinkelfiend's side. Let's see if we cannot find ways to continue irritating him."

"As you wish," said Rupert, "but I can't see how irritating my father will shift him from his goal, old friend. Father's very determined and powerful. He won't hold back much longer. He's going to continue to bring back Vlad Dracula, and his task will be that much easier with us out of the way – *and* he still has the dagger."

"All the more reason as to why we must act," said Helsing. "I feel Sprantz could be the key to our problem. I think he must be in with Krinkelfiend's plans. I am determined to find him."

"Remember that he is determined to find *you*, too," warned Inspector Klaw.

"I will be very careful, have no fear," Helsing assured him. "And to that end, I could use your help. If we leave the crypt one by one and spread around town, one of us might spot him. We can meet back here in two hours' time and discuss our findings."

"Very well," said Klaw, although he was unsure how much it would achieve.

Helsing decided to go home, make himself something to eat and drink, then put his feet up for half an hour. His home was in a street made up solely of terraced houses, with fields at the back. It was through the fields that Helsing chose to reach his home that morning, hoping to arrive there undetected.

He tiptoed inside and did a quick and thorough

search of the abode, satisfying himself that no one was there or had been there at an earlier time.

He moved to each of his windows in turn – including the one Rupert had broken during his unorthodox but timely arrival – and peeped through the curtains. No sign of a spy, not that a good spy would allow himself to be visible: but Helsing knew the telltale signs: sunlight flashing on the lenses of field glasses, and trampled grass where someone had gone to find a suitable hiding place.

He moved to a side window which overlooked his small patch of garden. His gardener, Abelesk, back turned to the house, was busy tending the plants. Other than Abelesk, there was no one to see and nothing out of the ordinary.

Helsing sighed, satisfied with his check, and sat down in an armchair to take a few minutes' rest before contemplating his next move. Soon he had dozed off, exhausted by the last twenty-four hours of adventure.

Abelesk, who wasn't Abelesk but Sprantz in disguise, turned around slowly and moved towards the unlocked back door, letting himself in without making a sound. He reached into the inside pocket of his grubby workman's shirt and produced a long hypodermic syringe. With an evil smile spreading across his lined, bony face, he rammed the needle into the back of Helsing's neck and forced the chemical into the old man's veins. Helsing let out a muted moan before keeling over to one side in a deep, comatose sleep.

"Have a nice rest, old man," whispered Sprantz. He dashed to the front door and whistled once. Three men in white overalls bearing a stretcher appeared. "Over there," said Sprantz. "He's unconscious, so he won't cause you any trouble between here and Rimpton."

On leaving the crypt, Inspector Klaw wandered the streets aimlessly. After half an hour, he decided he would be of greater use keeping a secret eye on Helsing. He was worried about the old man. It had been made clear that Sprantz was trying to get him locked away at Rimpton, so *some*one had to look out for him.

Bran is not a large town, and Klaw thought he would soon come across Helsing. But he didn't. Luckily, Helsing had told the inspector where he lived so Klaw decided to pay a visit.

Discovering Helsing's front door unlocked was the first sign Klaw had that things were not as they should be. The second sign was a strange moaning noise coming from somewhere in the garden.

Inspector Klaw rushed across the lawn and into the potting shed. He found a man there, bound and gagged and secured to a heavy table. He was wearing nothing but his underwear. Klaw pulled the gag from his mouth. "They attacked me!" gasped the man.

"Who attacked you?" asked Klaw.

"I don't know, exactly. There were three or four of them."

"Who are you?" asked Klaw.

"I'm a gardener," replied the man. "My name is Abelesk. I do a bit of work for Herr Helsing."

"Could it be that Sprantz has struck?" wondered Klaw. "If so, then poor Helsing has most likely been taken to Rimpton. That was what Sprantz wanted for Helsing."

Klaw quickly freed the man before dashing back through the house and into the street. He had to find the others and tell them his news.

Closed wrought iron gates with the word "Asylum"
scrawled across a piece of board marked the entrance.

❧ Chapter Ten
Rimpton, from the Inside

But as it turned out, Inspector Klaw couldn't find Rupert or the professor, and had to wait until his friends had gathered back in the crypt before he could tell them what he feared had become of Helsing.

"Rimpton!" cried Rupert in horror. "Then we must go there at once."

They waved down a landau in the high street and climbed aboard. "Where to, gentlemen?" asked the cabbie.

"Rimpton!" replied Klaw.

The cabbie gave a little shiver, said nothing and drove them towards Rimpton.

The landau pulled up some twenty feet short of a long, high wall, which was the boundary to Rimpton. One set of closed wrought iron gates with the word "Asylum" scrawled in red paint across a piece of board marked the main entrance to the institution.

Inspector Klaw paid the driver and told him to wait for their return. "And when we *do* return," he said, "we might be in a bit of a hurry, so let's look sharp, eh?"

"You're the boss," smiled the driver, who picked up his newspaper and settled down in his seat.

"I'm not certain he's even going to wait for us," whispered Rupert, as he helped the professor down from the running-board. "He probably thinks we're inmates."

The cabbie shook his head slowly a couple of times and sneered. "They should never have let that lot out in the first place," he told his horses, who naturally had nothing to say on the matter.

Rimpton was as grim as its name suggested. As the men moved gingerly through the gates, Klaw turned to the others, "Wait here," he said. "We don't want to arouse too much suspicion."

A few minutes later, Klaw found the opportunity he was looking for. He waved to the others, signalling them to join him at a window through which he was peering inside the building.

"Empty room," he whispered.

"That's because no one is in it," said Orlov, seriously.

"Yes, Orlov," said Klaw, patiently, "and because it is empty, we can enter the building through this window."

With that, Klaw heaved the sash window up and jumped into the room, followed quickly by the others. Orlov tripped over his bad leg and rolled to the floor shouting, "OUCH!" which brought a response of "Ssh!" from the other three.

"Into the spider's web we go," whispered the professor enthusiastically.

"I should have stayed at Castle Bran," moaned Orlov.

"Come, dear boy," said the professor, "surely you want to get better?"

The thought of a new body made Orlov smile, though with his twisted and swollen lips, smiling seemed a painful, rather than pleasurable, experience.

"This room," said Rupert quietly, "seems to have been empty for a long time."

"That's because there's nothing in it," said Orlov.

"Please be quiet a moment, Orlov," said Rupert. "It's a large building," he went on, "so presumably parts of it are not used." He nodded at the door which was shut. "Let's move on."

Beyond the door came the tip-tap sound of crisp footfalls. The noise grew loud, then quieter, until fading away altogether.

"Safe now," said Rupert, softly prising open the door.

They stepped out and entered a long corridor. It was poorly lit and very sombre. There was a little light coming in through two or three windows. The windows were nearly twelve feet from the floor, so preventing anyone from making an escape.

"Left or right?" said Rupert.

"We could split up," said Klaw.

"A little dangerous, Inspector," said the professor. "If something happens to one of us, how will the others be warned?"

"A good point, Professor," said Klaw. Suddenly, he

snapped his fingers. "I've got it. What we need to do is dress up in white coats like doctors and nurses. That way no one will question us and we can move around freely."

"Then we should turn left," said the professor.

"Why left?" asked Klaw.

The professor pointed at a sign hanging above a door further down the corridor. It read: *Laundry Room*.

A loud, agonizing cry came echoing towards them, and they shuddered in their shoes. "Another patient receiving 'treatment'," winced Rupert.

"Let us hope it isn't our dear friend, Helsing," said the professor.

"Let's hurry up and find him and get out of here," said Orlov. For once, none of them disagreed with him.

Finding white coats proved easier than finding Helsing. Orlov, they decided, could assist them by posing as a patient. As Rupert explained to him, "It's easier to believe you're a patient than a member of the staff."

"Thanks very much," frowned Orlov.

They trundled down numerous corridors with Orlov between them, fidgeting and ranting and raving and playing his role rather well.

They passed many staff and hardly caused a glance. "This appears to be working," whispered Klaw.

"It's all right for you," complained Orlov. "You've got the easy role."

On a whim, the professor stopped one of the nurses. She was big and strong, and looked capable of dealing with any trouble on the premises.

"Excuse me," said the professor, "could you tell me where the new arrival is? This one's to be put with him. They're associates."

"Which new arrival are you referring to?" asked the nurse. "We've had three today."

"Herr Helsing," said the professor.

She eyed the professor and his other white-coated colleagues with interest a moment, then studied the grotesque features of Orlov. The name Helsing had clearly struck home more soundly than the professor had expected or wanted.

"Where did you find *this* creature?" she asked, nodding at Orlov.

"Bran," replied the professor. "Lost and walking the streets, poor thing. No doubt we will do all we can for him during his stay."

The nurse laughed heartily at that. "That's a good one, Doctor," she said, continuing to chuckle for some while. "The Herr Direktor will do something for him, all right. This one will be in the Death Room before he can say 'Boo'!"

"Ah, the Death Room," said the professor, as though he knew exactly what she was talking about.

"Yes," said the nurse, "along with that Helsing you mentioned."

With a brisk, "Good morning, gentlemen," she marched off like a runaway train.

"I don't like the sound of the Death Room," remarked Orlov.

"I imagine that is the general idea," said the professor, with his usual display of studious calm.

"Where to now?" said Rupert as the corridor came to an end and they were forced to choose left or right.

"The Death Room, I presume," said the professor.

"That's if we can find it," said Klaw.

"If we do, then I'll just wait outside," said Orlov.

A loud and terrible scream – the second since their arrival – reached their ears and made them tremble.

"That could be what we're looking for," said the professor.

"The scream?" said Klaw.

"The scream," nodded the professor. "Most people would scream if they found themselves in a room called the Death Room, would they not?"

"He has a point," said Rupert, leading the way.

Another scream followed. "Behind that door," said Klaw, rushing towards a door that had a skull and crossbones sign hanging from it, and beneath it the words: "NO ADMITTANCE TO ANYONE WITHOUT PRIOR ARRANGEMENT WITH THE DIREKTOR."

Klaw and Rupert burst through the door simultaneously, closely followed by the professor, but less closely followed by Orlov, who peered anxiously around the door's frame before entering.

The sight that confronted them left them somewhat perplexed. The screams had not come from Helsing, but from the male nurses that Helsing was in the process of securing with lengths of rope.

"Gentlemen, what a surprise," smiled Helsing. From the way he greeted them, they could have walked into his favourite inn.

"But... But..." began Klaw.

"The Death Room!" gasped Rupert. "We thought you were in it."

"I am," nodded Helsing. "Indeed, we all are. This is it."

"You are a rare creature, Herr Helsing," chuckled the professor. "You must have had some help to manage all this," he said, gesturing at the three nurses who were tied up back to back. "Either that, or there is much more to you than any of us understand!"

Helsing raised his eyes at the professor, and smiled, but said nothing.

"Now Helsing's safe," said Orlov, "I want a beautiful face and body like Rupert promised. And the only way I'm going to get it is through the dagger."

"Yes, yes, yes," said Rupert, "we've discussed all that before. All in good time, Orlov. First things first."

"Quite," said the professor. "For a start, does anyone know how we are going to get away from this place?"

"I do," growled Sprantz, appearing at the door like a ghost, his grizzled hair flowing behind him like strips of wire. "But I shall *not* be telling you, my dear, fresh inmates of the Rimpton Asylum."

*The vampire was none other than the vampire:
Vlad Dracula himself.*

♯ Chapter Eleven
Rupert and the Dagger

hat now?" sighed Inspector Klaw, as he sat with his companions in a dank cell beneath the asylum. "I'm growing very tired of moving from one cell to another," Klaw went on, staring through the single, barred window. "I'm a policeman: it is supposed to be *me* who does the locking up."

"Just think how much the cab fare is going to cost if that driver's still waiting out front," said Orlov, stupidly.

"Don't be absurd, Orlov," said Rupert heavily. "And anyway, paying for it won't be our problem if we don't get out of here."

"Outside, the darkness approaches," said Klaw, "and Krinkelfiend will be awakening. Perhaps even Dracula himself tonight."

"I think we need to be a little calmer, gentlemen," suggested Rupert. "We mustn't forget that I am not without a few vampire tricks. Indeed, I'm sure I could get us out of here this minute," he said. "It's more a question of whether it is appropriate to escape at present."

"I think it's *very* appropriate to escape at present," said Orlov.

"The thing is," Rupert went on, as if talking to himself, "should I turn into a bat and fly through the night to Castle Bran? Or, better still, should I click my fingers at the bars on the window, allowing us all to escape? Or, should you – and I personally believe this to be the best choice – all remain here as prisoners, while I attempt to do something about getting the dagger away from Father? Or to put it another way, while I attempt to get Father away from the dagger, which, though tricky enough, might prove the easier of the two. The dagger, we know from our earlier experience, intends to go nowhere with us."

"If you really could contain your father," said the professor thoughtfully, "it would certainly prevent him from bringing Dracula back."

"But why go alone when we could *all* escape?" asked Klaw.

"Because they do not know we can all escape," answered Helsing, smiling. "Our friend here is quite right in what he proposes. The only time we will arouse any suspicion is if it is found we have escaped. But for Rupert to go – that would be different. I doubt Sprantz will be back now he thinks we're taken care of, and the staff won't notice one missing person, especially when there is no sign to show how he could have escaped."

About an hour later, Rupert circled the dark turrets of Dracula's home.

He remained in bat form until he found an open window on the second floor, for it was here that his father kept the dagger hidden in the room with the secret cubbyhole. He circled a while longer, just to make sure his father wasn't prowling around the castle. Then he flew inside, the usual puff of purple smoke announcing his change into human form.

Treading softly, he moved along the open, crumbled corridor, the moonlight guiding him towards the room. Inside, it was just possible to see the panel on the mahogany wall.

"Wonderful!" whispered Rupert. "Perfect conditions for trying out my new plan. He thought it a clever plan, because he knew the dagger wouldn't let any mere mortal take it away from the castle – especially *this* castle. What he proposed to do was to use his reinstated powers to float the dagger through the air while he was in bat form. That way, no one would have to touch the dagger, so preventing it from protecting itself – he hoped.

The panel sank back into the wall at his touch, and there lay the dagger in its sheath, just as before. This time, he knew he must not fail.

As he prepared a special spell, he felt rather than saw another presence in the murky room. Annoyed at being caught, he turned stiffly, expecting to be confronted by his father making all kinds of nasty threats. Instead, he saw the dark outline against the open doorway of someone he didn't know, yet in a way that he couldn't explain, knew perfectly well.

The figure was tall – very tall – and wore a black top hat and cape: indeed, he was very similar to his father in appearance. He seemed inexplicably distinguished. The moon appeared from behind a passing cloud, and Rupert could see his skin was transparently thin. There was an aura about this silent visitor which Rupert found quite overwhelming. More overwhelming was the understanding – in the split-second it took the moon to illuminate his dead face – that this vampire was none other than *the* vampire: Vlad Dracula himself.

Arnold Krinkelfiend climbed out of his coffin and stretched. He had never been very good at getting up first thing at night.

He poured himself a glass of port and began thinking about the night ahead. Then his eyes fell upon a note on the floor. It was from Sprantz: "Have all hostages at Rimpton (including Rupert). Await your instructions."

"Excellent, Sprantz," said Krinkelfiend, rubbing his hands together as he always did when he was either pleased or excited – or both, as he was now. "You'll definitely get my vote for another term as mayor."

Krinkelfiend took to the air – unaware, naturally, that his son and his lord and master were facing each other in the presence of the dagger inside the castle.

Rupert wasn't sure if he should speak or just wait for Dracula to make the first move.

After what seemed an eternity, the vampire spoke at last.

"Who are you, and what are you doing in my castle?"

They were the obvious questions, of course, yet Rupert didn't know how to answer, bearing in mind that to reply truthfully could have devastating results. And wouldn't Dracula know if he was lying? Didn't he have the power to know everything?

"I'm Arnold Krinkelfiend's son," Rupert explained in a voice he hardly recognized as being his own. "My father brought the dagger here to bring you back to mortal life. It looks like he succeeded." He smiled cheerfully, trying to win the vampire's trust.

"No one brought me back to life," said Dracula. "I chose to return."

"I thought that involved a ceremony?" asked Rupert, confused by his response.

Dracula didn't answer. He stretched out a hand, and for a moment Rupert mistakenly thought he wanted him to shake it. But as he watched, the arm grew longer and longer, until it stretched the length of the room, picked up the dagger and sheath, then returned itself to its normal length.

That was a trick which would have impressed even his father, thought Rupert.

"I know about Count Arnold Krinkelfiend," Dracula said suddenly, in a voice that was disturbingly monotonous and melancholy. "He disturbed my rest once before. He is a fool, and of no use to me."

"He is a bit silly at times," agreed Rupert, uncomfortably. "But he thought he was being of some help. I don't think he realized you could reappear in mortal form whenever you saw fit."

"Where is he now?" asked Dracula.

"I imagine he's on his way to Rimpton," said Rupert. "An asylum a few miles north of here. He is holding my friends there, and will want to check

149

up on them. We've caused him quite a bit of discomfort over the years."

Dracula waved a hand through the air and at once Arnold Krinkelfiend appeared, flapping his arms and wondering what on earth was happening. He changed from bat to man, and fell to the floor in a messy, confused heap. "Wh-what? How?" Then he saw his son. "So, it is *you*!" he snarled. "What trickery is this? And who is this you have brought...?"

"Be silent!" said Dracula, and the authority in his voice made Krinkelfiend do as he was commanded.

"Hello, Father," said Rupert through a sickly smile. "I'd ... er ... like you to meet Dracula, or Vlad Dracul, or Vlad Tepes, or whatever you prefer, really. He's decided to come back and see his castle."

Krinkelfiend fell to his feet and began kissing the vampire's shoes. "My lord and master!" he cried. "How I have waited for this moment. I had prepared a ceremony for you, but ... but being the genius you are, you are able to return to us, your humble servants, unassisted. It is truly an amazing moment."

"You are drooling over my shoes," stated Dracula, in the even voice that revealed none of his inner feelings.

"Oh, sorry," apologized Krinkelfiend, rubbing them clean with his sleeve before clambering back to his feet.

"You are both vampires?" asked Dracula, though it was more a statement of a fact.

"Yes," said Krinkelfiend, and Rupert was extremely grateful his father had included him in this description. Maybe he *did* still care for him, just a bit.

"This pleases me."

Both of them heaved a sigh of relief at hearing this.

"But you must understand that I have no need for you. You may leave and go about your business of the dark, but do not disturb me here again. I have returned after centuries of rest to do my work alone. I will always work alone. Go freely."

Krinkelfiend looked quite stunned. "But I've arranged a great following from the graveyard in Bran," he explained. "We all are here to serve you. Others will follow, just as it has been written."

"My work has changed," said the vampire. "In my mortal time, my armies proved disappointing. I do not wish to have followers any more. I will work and exist alone. No one must visit me. Orlov will be unfrozen, and he will serve all my needs."

Krinkelfiend shuffled awkwardly. "Ah, yes," he said. "Er ... about Orlov, lord and master..."

Dracula raised his head a notch, and Rupert glimpsed the cold, unblinking eyes.

"What of Orlov?"

"Knowing the history of Castle Bran," Rupert explained, deciding to help his father out, "when we arrived here we went to see if he was all right, but we found he was ... well ... gone."

"That's right," nodded Krinkelfiend, vigorously. "Gone. Not a sign of him. He must have defrosted during a heat wave or something."

"Yes, that must be it," said Rupert.

Dracula looked from one to the other, then said, "I hope your words are not laced with deceit. Anyone who proves to be a traitor – vampire or mortal – will be impaled. I, Vlad Tepes, promise this."

Rupert and his father shrugged their shoulders. "We could take another look?" suggested Rupert.

"Go now," said Dracula. "Return to your homeland and do your work of the night. I wish to think. I wish to be alone."

"As you wish," bowed Krinkelfiend, and at once

turned into a bat and flew from the room, quickly followed by another bat. But Rupert didn't make it to the doorway.

"Not you," commanded Dracula, holding him by a wing. "As Orlov has mysteriously disappeared, *you* will serve me as Orlov once did."

Krinkelfiend heard the words and felt a pang of envy that it should be his son – in truth, only a *half*-vampire, and a poor one at that – who should remain to serve his Lord and Master. Rupert, on the other hand, began wondering how on earth he was ever going to get out of the dreadful fix he now found himself in.

As Krinkelfiend flew again towards Rimpton, he had a sudden idea and cried out in the night air, "Orlov. I must return Orlov to him. Then my former son will be revealed as a charlatan. And I must make sure my lord and master thinks it was Rupert who interfered with Orlov's frozen grave. Once that has been done, I will see to it that Orlov comes to some harm, then I will be our lord and master's sole servant. I haven't done all this to be superseded by my interfering son!" Krinkelfiend's mad laugh echoed through the dark skies.

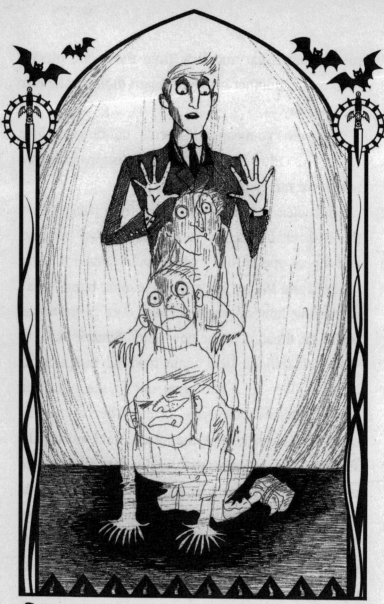

Orlov looked at his hands, then felt his smooth face and flaxen hair. "I am beautiful!" he cried.

☙ Chapter Twelve
Double Trouble

Helsing, Orlov, Professor von Morcumstein and Inspector Klaw were dozing fitfully in their uncomfortable room inside Rimpton as the night wore on. Suddenly Helsing stiffened, aware that something was not right. "What is it, Herr Helsing?" asked the professor, rubbing his sleepy eyes and noticing the sudden change in the man.

"I'm not sure," said Helsing, "but I feel my past

catching up with me. Something lurks outside these walls which causes me great turmoil within."

"Something lurks *inside* these walls which upsets me!" moaned Orlov.

"Perhaps Rupert is in trouble," said Klaw, overhearing them talk.

"Yes. Perhaps that is it," said Helsing, knowing that it wasn't that simple. "I think we wait till dawn, and if Rupert hasn't returned we must consider taking matters into our own hands."

Count Krinkelfiend burst into Rimpton on foot. "Where's Sprantz?" he demanded of the first member of staff he came across.

"He's gone to interview the new arrivals," said the man, and he gave the appropriate directions.

Sprantz had only just entered the room where Helsing and his colleagues were being held, when Krinkelfiend stormed in.

"I need Orlov," he said, striding over and grabbing the terrified Orlov by the collar.

"Don't look so pathetic," said Krinkelfiend. "I need your help on this occasion, though nothing would have given me greater pleasure than to blast you into a million tiny fragments."

Sensing a reprieve, but without understanding why, Orlov smiled hastily up at his former master. "It's so good to see you, Master," he cringed. "I hit my head on something, lost my memory and..."

"Stop snivelling, Orlov," said Krinkelfiend. "Someone has returned to his castle. He is eager to see you."

"Vlad Dracula has returned?" said Helsing, eyeing the count for the first time. "Then it seems he didn't require your help after all."

"Be silent, you old fool," said Krinkelfiend, "or I'll ... or I'll..."

"You know as well as I that any 'or I'll's are out of the question," said Helsing. The professor and Klaw exchanged confused looks. Why was Helsing so unconcerned about Krinkelfiend's threats?

"Look here, Helsing," said Krinkelfiend, beginning to go red in the face – quite a rare feat for a bloodless vampire – "you've caused him enough trouble over the centuries. Don't you ever get bored of causing trouble?"

"No, never!" smiled Helsing. "Causing vampires trouble is my sole purpose in life."

"Just because you happen to know my lord and master personally, doesn't make *you* special, Helsing," said Krinkelfiend.

"He *knows* Dracula!" gasped the professor to Klaw.

"I have never claimed to be special," said Helsing. "Just more special than *you*!"

Krinkelfiend seemed on the point of explosion when Sprantz stepped forward. "What... What do you wish me to do?" asked Sprantz, as confused by all these goings-on as Klaw and the professor.

"I don't know," shrugged Krinkelfiend. "Do what you always do."

"But these people. Shall I release them?"

Krinkelfiend thought a moment. "Arrange a coach to deliver them at once to Castle Bran," he told him. "Let's see what our lord and master makes of them."

With that, he grabbed Orlov by the scruff of the neck and, turning into bat form, took to the air.

"Help!" cried Orlov. Krinkelfiend whispered a spell and the walls of the room parted magically to let them through. "I'm scared of heights!"

The castle appeared empty when Krinkelfiend returned there with Orlov.

"Where can he be?" Krinkelfiend wondered aloud as they traipsed along the dark corridors.

"Oh well, never mind," said Orlov, turning to leave. "We'll try again another night."

"Not so fast, Orlov," said Krinkelfiend, pulling him back. "You've got a job to do!"

Suddenly a voice came from behind Krinkelfiend.

"You return here uninvited," he stated. Krinkelfiend jumped, having not noticed the arrival of his lord and master.

"Oh yes, my apologies, lord and master," bowed Krinkelfiend. "Please excuse this intrusion, but I've found Orlov. It seems my son, Rupert, freed him and took him to use as his own servant."

"No he didn't," whispered Orlov, who received a hefty kick in the shins from Krinkelfiend.

"So, Orlov," growled Dracula. "We are together again. It is like old times, is it not?"

"Yes, master," bowed Orlov. "Welcome back to life, my lord!"

"You may leave us now," ordered Dracula, looking directly at Krinkelfiend.

"But... But I thought you may need me ... now you've discovered my son's treachery, and..."

"Your son, Rupert, will be dealt with as and when I choose. It is intruders I dislike," he told him. "Take yourself from these parts – make yourself a new home; a new existence. And remain patient, for one day I may require you."

Krinkelfiend promptly bowed again, took to the air and left the castle. After a few minutes of flying, he landed in a field and turned back into human form. "This is all Rupert's fault!" he cried to the emptiness around him. "I'll... I'll..." he began frustratedly. He pulled off his top hat and stamped on it several times, which didn't really make him feel much better. The rejection of his lord and master was proving too much to bear.

But as quickly as he'd begun sobbing, he stopped. A wicked grin grew on his lips. "The dagger!" he gasped. "If I had the dagger, everyone would listen to me. *Even* my lord and master."

Back in the castle, Orlov waited to see what

Dracula would say next. He was somewhat surprised when the vampire's words were, "Thank goodness he's gone!" and began rubbing his hands and laughing. Then there was a burst of purple smoke, and in front of Orlov stood not Dracula, but Rupert.

"Don't look so surprised, Orlov," smiled Rupert. "I do have *some* powers of my own."

"You... You're not...?"

"Dracula? No, I'm not, Orlov. I'm Rupert, as you can see. The art of cloaking requires the vampire to touch the object it wishes to become. I managed to brush past Dracula earlier this evening, and *whoosh* – a quick spell and here, as far as you and my father were concerned, stood Dracula. Mind you," he added, "I don't think I could have kept it up for much longer."

"Where's the real thing?" asked Orlov, taking nervous glances all around and above him.

"Out hunting," replied Rupert. "That's what he told me, at least. Don't look so worried. I can't imagine he will return before dawn; not after hundreds of years of rest and solitude."

"What now?"

"Now, Orlov," said Rupert, "I prove that I am not someone who breaks a promise. The moment is now right."

He led a bemused Orlov to the room with the cubbyhole. Without touching the dagger, Rupert stared deeply into the Burmese ruby. "Whatever happens, Orlov, be sure I will do my best."

"That doesn't sound very promising," said Orlov.

Ignoring him, Rupert began a strange chant, and slowly the jewel glowed in the dark. Orlov watched a little impatiently. Though it was all very interesting, he couldn't see it doing much for him.

But then he felt a mighty pain shoot right through his whole being. So powerful was the pain it tossed him to the floor as if he'd been struck by a bolt of lightning.

He slowly climbed to his knees, feeling decidedly groggy.

"Who ran over me?" he groaned.

"Orlov," smiled Rupert. "You'll never have to worry about looking in a mirror again."

Orlov looked at his hands, then felt his smooth face and flaxen hair. "I am beautiful!" he cried. "And my mind is clear. I understand things. I can sense it. All my fears have left me."

"A little modesty, please, Orlov," laughed Rupert.

As Orlov continued to praise himself, Rupert moved to the passageway that overlooked the open courtyard. Down below he'd heard the arrival of a carriage.

"Who can this be?" he wondered aloud.

"Oh, it's all right," said the handsome Orlov, striding across the room towards the doorway. "It's Helsing and the others. Krinkelfiend ordered them to be dropped here."

"How considerate," chuckled Rupert. "Come, my friend. For the moment our work is done. And thanks to the carriage below, we have the means to make a hasty departure."

"What about the dagger?" asked Orlov, reluctant to leave it behind.

"I hardly dare touch it," said Rupert. "It proved a little unstable the last time I put my hands upon it."

"Well, we can't leave it here. Dracula mustn't keep it. He's mad enough as it is. If the dagger is as powerful as you all assume, we'll pay a high price for leaving it behind."

"Then allow me," said a voice, and behind Orlov Rupert saw the swooping figure of Krinkelfiend in bat-form enter the room and snatch the dagger and sheath from the cubbyhole before swiftly disappearing into the night.

"FATHER!" cried Rupert.

"Well, that's torn it," sighed Orlov.

"I'll have to go after him."

"Hello?" called a voice from down below.

Rupert peered down at the courtyard through the dim light that issued from the wall torches and saw that it was Karl Sprantz, the mayor.

"Hello there," Rupert called back, then snapped his fingers, turning Sprantz into a frog. Then he and Orlov made their way down into the courtyard where Rupert placed the frog in his pocket. "Ugh! I didn't mean to make you so slimy!" he remarked.

Just then, Helsing emerged from the coach.

"We're coming to join you, Helsing," called Rupert. "Wait there!"

"Who is the tall young man at your side?" shouted Helsing, peering through the night.

"Meet the new Orlov!" smiled Rupert.

"Judging by Orlov's handsome features, I take it we have the dagger?" said Helsing.

"Ah," sighed Rupert as they reached the coach. "I'm afraid there's still work to be done there. Give me a few minutes, will you? Perhaps meanwhile you can explain to our professor and the inspector here, a little of your fascinating history. I think they deserve to know."

"My feelings entirely," agreed Helsing. "But you take care, Rupert. Your father is always at his most dangerous when he feels everyone is against him."

Helsing turned to the new Orlov. "Into the coach, my friend."

"My, my, Orlov," said the professor, as Orlov climbed in and sat down next to him. "Beauty treatment indeed!"

"It can't be Orlov!" gasped Inspector Klaw.

"It is indeed," said Orlov, with a smile.

"Now, Helsing," said the professor, "I believe I heard Rupert mention something about your fascinating past?"

"Yes, well..." began Helsing, who then began to recount his long life as an Immortal.

This was no ordinary colossal dragon; it was one with two giant heads.

⚔ Chapter Thirteen
The Clash of the Vampires

While Helsing told his remarkable story, Rupert tracked down his father to a field just outside the castle grounds. Krinkelfiend was sitting on the grass, legs crossed, bathed in moonlight. The dagger in his hands twinkled. "Such beauty," he sighed. "And such power." Then he sensed, rather than saw, his son coming towards him and quickly leaped to his feet.

"There you are, Father," said Rupert, bursting

from bat into man. "We need to talk. I really don't think it's a sensible idea you hanging on to that dagger. Your lord and master is not going to be very happy when he discovers that you've—"

"Be silent!" spat Krinkelfiend. "This dagger will make me important to Vlad Dracula. I have not worked tirelessly to aid his return only to be dismissed with barely a word. It's my dagger – I found it. And if I go, it goes too. I will hide it, and only give it back to him when he has embraced me as his one and only servant and friend. As for you..."

"What about me, Father?" said Rupert.

"All my plans would have worked out if you and your meddling friends hadn't interfered. This is the second time you have poked your nose where it was not wanted," Krinkelfiend reminded him. "And it shall be the last!"

With that, the count began to expand and change shape. Rupert watched with growing alarm. "His powers have increased," he thought. "Goodness knows what he's planning. I *have* to get away from here!"

But Rupert didn't have a chance to go anywhere.

He tried in vain to transform into a bat, but his father must have put a spell on him, making him unable to change into *any*thing. Rupert looked up to see what his father was up to, and wished he hadn't. His father was taking the shape of a colossal dragon – twenty feet tall. But this was no ordinary colossal dragon; it was one with *two* giant heads.

A burst of fire sprayed from the dragon's nostrils almost roasting Rupert on the spot. Just in time, Rupert threw himself to the ground, rolling over and over.

Again there was a rush of heat near Rupert's body, and he twisted and turned, barely managing to keep a couple of feet ahead of the deadly flames. This was tiring work – he had to do something or soon his father would overcome him and then he would be roasted!

"Father, you must calm yourself!" Rupert called out desperately, but his pleas were lost in the hissing and smoking of the dragon's giant nostrils. Then the dragon took a mighty swing at Rupert with a green clawed foot, narrowly missing his head and hitting the ground instead, leaving a deep trail of torn earth.

"This is getting very dangerous," thought Rupert, putting it somewhat mildly.

Dodging the blows and trying to escape was not the answer: soon his father would connect with one of his powerful blows, or one of the bursts of fire from his furnace-like nostrils, and that would be the end of Rupert. "Father," Rupert pleaded again, "please stop this!"

But the dragon's eyes turned huge and red.

"You thought you could get the better of me?" growled his father scornfully. "Me, the mighty Count Arnold Krinkelfiend?"

"I do think you need to control your temper a bit, Father," Rupert suggested nervously, trying to catch his breath.

"Enough talking!" said the dragon, raising its claws menacingly above Rupert's bruised and battered head. "It is time to finish this right now. Prepare yourself for a very painful end."

But before Krinkelfiend could do anything at all to his son, a bolt of blue lightning shot from the distant turret of the castle and struck the dragon right in its chest. With a mighty yelp, the dragon dissolved. In its place stood Count Krinkelfiend, rubbing his smoking clothes. And beside him, on the ground, lay the dagger.

"What... What happened?" he asked, and his voice was timid and shaky; nothing like the commanding Krinkelfiend voice of moments before.

"Er, behind you, Father," said Rupert.

Krinkelfiend turned. There stood the dark, menacing figure of Count Vlad Dracula.

"Oh, er, good evening, my lord and master," began Krinkelfiend. "I, er, was just having a talk with my son..."

"I will not permit one vampire to kill another vampire," Dracula told him. "Whatever the reason," he added.

Rupert shuffled uneasily. He wasn't sure which was worse: facing his father as a dragon, or facing the master of all vampires.

"Go now, both of you!" ordered Dracula. "And beware that if ever I catch you behaving in such a way again, I will not be so lenient."

"Oh, right. Yes... Yes, we understand," stammered Rupert.

Dracula stretched out an arm about six feet, picked up the fallen dagger, burst into smoke and was gone.

Alone again with his son, Krinkelfiend raised his hands, a dangerous spell on the tips of his fingers. "Why, you meddling fool! You've done it again – you've ruined everything. It will take me ages to win back my lord and master's trust. I'll... I'll... I'll..." Krinkelfiend's fingers began to quiver.

"Tut, tut, Father," said Rupert. "Do you want your master to become even angrier with you?"

"I'll... I'll..." continued Krinkelfiend, but with less conviction. He realized his son was right. There was nothing he could do without further angering Vlad Dracula.

In a mighty burst of purple smoke, Count Krinkelfiend transformed into a bat and hovered just in front of Rupert, "Don't think you have seen the last of me!" he spat. "I'll be back!" And with that he shot off into the night.

"I'm sure you will, Father," Rupert mused to

himself. "And I expect we'll be here to greet you. But I don't even want to think about that now..."

Tired and battered, he returned to his friends.

"We were growing worried about you," wheezed Helsing. "You were gone so long."

"I'm all right," said Rupert, struggling up to the landau.

"Who has the dagger?" asked the professor.

"Vlad Dracula," replied Rupert.

"Does that mean we have lost?" asked Orlov.

"Not entirely," said Rupert. "Father went running off with his tail between his legs, vowing to return. But at least we upset all his plans."

"And we are alive to fight another day, should Dracula prove troublesome," said Klaw.

"And if he does," said Helsing, "he knows he will have *me* breathing down his neck."

"Then, at least for the time being, let's go home," said Klaw. "PLEASE!"

"You all go ahead," said Rupert. "I've two more visits to make."

"To whom?" asked Helsing.

"The first is to Schleck. The poor shepherd is still

made of stone. I have more than enough of my old powers back to break that spell."

"And who is the other you intend to visit?" asked Klaw.

"Not *who*," smiled Rupert, "but *what*!"

Epilogue

Extract from the *Bran Times*

*I*t is not known how the fire at Rimpton Asylum was started, but it is remarkable that, apart from minor cuts and bruises, no one appears to have been hurt.

Those members of staff interviewed have described witnessing a giant bat flying across the roof of the asylum, followed shortly by a massive fireball. The Direktor of the Institute says it is highly unlikely that any of the patients, all of whom made a quick escape, will ever be found. He also states that there are no immediate plans to rebuild the asylum, and accepts that he has probably been forced into early retirement.

The mayor of Bran, Karl Sprantz, was arrested at the scene of the fire by local police. He has been charged with corruption and, if found guilty, faces immediate dismissal from office and a lengthy jail sentence. The mayor appears to be suffering from delusions. He is insisting that he is a frog and is determined to spend the rest of his life in a large pond. "Had Rimpton not burned down last night," commented a spokesman, "then the former mayor would have been a prime candidate to take up residence there."

Follow the adventures of Rupert, Inspector Klaw,
Professor von Morcumstein and the count...

Watch out for the third part of the
Tall Tales of Dracula's Daggers:

Dracula's Revenge

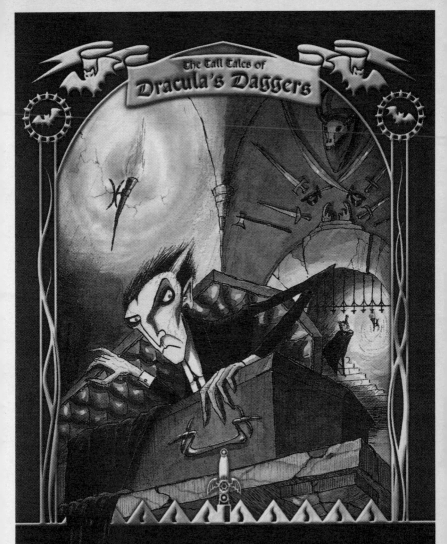

The Tall Tales of Dracula's Daggers

Dracula's Revenge

(In which an intruder in the crypt disturbs Vlad's kip…)

Gary Morecambe

SCHOLASTIC